Maria Lewis is from Hackney, London
She's a government officer by day, and
an aspiring novelist by night.
Her wish is that one day the novelist part can be by
day too.

Also by Maria Lewis

One Girl and 3 Guys

Jess finds herself in triple trouble with not one, not two but *three* guys. One won't let go of the commitment she doesn't want, another won't give her the commitment she *does* want and the third...well she's not sure *what* he wants! And to top it all, no one is taking no for an answer...

The Perfect Place

Gina's back! And now that her BIG secret is out of the bag, she just has to that ideal spot to make her secret a thing of the past. But where should that perfect place be? A sun kissed beach? Maybe a posh hotel? Or how about one of the 306 flights of stairs in the Shard? It's not long before Gina learns that there's more to 'losing' her secret than there was to keeping it!

What customers are saying:

"...didn't want it to finish..."
"...loved the characters! Can't wait for the next one!"
"...just too funny!"

The BIG Secret
Maria Lewis

Incorplus Publishing

First published in Great Britain in 2016 by Incorplus ltd

Copyright © Maria Lewis 2016

Maria Lewis has asserted her right under the Copyright, Design and Patents Act 1988 to be identified as the author of this work.

A CIP catalogue record for this book is available from the British Library

Typeset in 13pt Garamond

Printed and Bound in Great Britain

ISBN:

978-0-9560842-1-7 (Paperback)

978-0-9560842-2-4 (eBook)

978-1-0687532-1-3 (Hard Cover)

For my husband John-Mark
who has supported me (literally)
so that I could do less of what I had to do
(working 9 to 5 for the government)
and more of what I wanted to do
(working 9 to 5 writing this book!)

Special Dedication

Ricardo Jordan, a great friend and
source of unwavering
positivity & encouragement.
Taken from this world far too soon.

Acknowledgements

Cory Belfon who has always been there in the background cheering me on. You get first props second book around!

My constructively-criticising Beta readers, Lisa Mills, Brittany Glasgow and from all the way in Abu Dhabi - Deborah Harris. The finished article is what it is because of your honest opinions!

Rochelle Rhodes for being that cool chick helping me get through each work day so I could make it to each write night!

Lydia at Bookouture Publishers who took the time to write me a couple of lines that helped me reshape this book into this final version

My Dad, Reuben Lewis simply because he's 90 years old and still an amazing man!

Asama Shah for being a great friend and an even greater nag – you made sure I got the job done, for sure!

Too many names to mention all of you that have helped make this book happen simply by continually asking 'When is it coming out?' – Thank you all!

One

If I reached over and strangled him right now, would a jury really convict me? Or would being subjected to the spray of crumbs I'm experiencing every time this man takes a bite of his breadstick be considered justifiable provocation?

'... and yah, I went to Switzerland when I was ten and I was the first in my class to ski down the advanced slope on one ski, in fact, as I recall, it had never been done before...'

Do they do hair clips for men? Surely men aren't supposed to be constantly flicking their hair from their eyes?

'...and yah, I skydived off a cliff in California when I was fourteen – the youngest in my class in fact. Huffington Jones who was two years my senior *and* the Headmaster's son actually cried at the prospect of doing it! Haw! Haw!...'

He has rather a large forehead...is there such a thing as forehead reductions? There's clearly a need for it...

'...then at fifteen, I climbed Mount Rogan in East Wales – the shortest male to ever do it if I remember rightly...'

My face is hurting with all this smiling. I nod my head strategically every 15 to 20 seconds (so he doesn't notice the bits where I've temporarily zoned out) in acknowledgement of Harold's continuous regalia of achievement. I'm actually a little impressed – not about his Everest attempt at thirteen – but at how after 3 hours we're still recounting his teenage years. I look at his lips – they are quite thin – possibly to make up for his excessive forehead. His nose isn't overly large. I suppose considering the amount of hot air expelling from his mouth, he needs something of adequate size to draw the oxygen back in again.

My eyes wander over his person.

From his shirt, pink with high collars, quite nice as far as pink shirts go.

To his belt – big buckle, kind of Yee-hah Cowboy...doesn't really go with the shirt.

To his jeans – straight, fitted...actually, tight might be a more apt description.

To his...No freakin' way...! My chair screeches along the ground in my hurry to get up.

'Thanks for a great salad! I had a great time and we must do this again soon!' I cut him off mid-sentence, jump up, grab for his hand and shake it like a cocktail mixer.

He's speechless. This kind of throws me and I actually stop for a second as I didn't think him not talking was possible. Then the vision I saw before suddenly flashes before my eyes, and my concentration is back on high alert again. Harold jumps up too.

'Oh...um...er...yes, we should?' He sounds clearly confused. 'So I'll call you?' He raises an eyebrow in question.

I give my jaws that last extra ounce of stretch for my hugest smile ever, 'Oh, I know how busy you're going to be, being the fastest person to climb all 306 flights of stairs in the Shard, so I'll call you and we can have a celebratory lunch! On me!'

I back away quickly from the table and give him a big wave, happy in the thought that I got away with my sanity intact and that by the end of the day all this facial exercise will give me award win-ning cheekbones. I'm already digging into my bag for my phone to call my best friend Lisa...no; in fact, this requires a personal visit. It's not quite 2pm yet – If I hurry, I should catch Lisa on her break at Mr Shah's coffee shop. She is never going to believe what I just saw.

Two

'So what was wrong this time, Gina?'

Lisa is looking at me through narrowed eyes as if I deliberately find reasons to avoid dating. And that is so not true. I'm just that girl who always happens to meet *that* guy. You know the kind of guy I mean. The one that's just got a certain something that you don't want to experience more than once if you can help it.

'Lisa, this was something that was on display for all to see. In fact, you would have had something to say if I *hadn't* noticed.'

I'm feeling quite indignant that my best friend would think I'd premeditate a reason to not go out with someone.

'Sooo...nose too big? Eyes too small?' Lisa is smirking at me behind her glass of orange juice with bits. As if I'm the only one who would think that a man with tiny eyes is shifty.

'No, actually. Worse.' I start to study my nails to add effect.

'Worse than a big nose?' Lisa is now frowning with concentration, 'Star trek Meekon forehead? Buck teeth? Bow legs?'

I shake my head at all her suggestions and start inspecting my 3-day-still-intact-manicure again. She'll crack in a minute – Lisa is never one for playing the long guessing game. I know I should just tell her, but I'm letting her stew for a bit as punishment for insinuating that I deliberately curtailed a date before hearing that my reasons for running a mile from this guy were absolutely, *categorically* necessary. I beckon towards the waiter station and two of them rush over at the same time, pushing one another in their efforts to get to the table.

'Can I help you, Madam?' Waiter one says, slightly out of breath.

'No, can *I* help you, Madam?' Waiter two edges his shoulder in front of Waiter one.

'It's fine I can deal with this customer. Don't you have to serve table 9?' Waiter one gives Waiter two a dirty look

'Table 9 is fine and I was already making my way to get this customer's order so you can make your way back to the kitchen...' Waiter two ignores Waiter one and gives me a big smile.

'And I shall, with *this* lady's order.' Waiter one edges his shoulder back in front.

I watch mesmerised as both the waiters start bickering with each other as to who will get the order. It's so rare to see such dedicated customer service these days.

'Guys!' Lisa shouts. Both waiters jump in surprise and stop talking.

'You' she points to Waiter one 'can get the lady a peppermint tea. And you' she points to Waiter two 'can get the lady a slice of apple pie with custard, not cream.'

Both waiters start bowing towards Lisa and rush off still shoving one another in their eagerness to get the order.

'Lisa, I don't like custard...'

'And you' Lisa jabs that finger at me 'had better tell me right now what was wrong with your date?' Yep. Lisa hates suspense. As she leans forward, I can see the desperation for knowledge in the whites of her eyes. I stare at her intensely for a few more seconds and slowly interlock my fingers. Just a few more seconds...

'NOW!' Lisa shouts

'Shoes.' I state succinctly.

'Shoes?' Lisa crinkles her face in confusion, 'What about his shoes? Didn't he have any? Did he come to lunch in bare feet or something?'

'White. Patent *and* Suede with crocodile-skin squares around the heel. Pointed – like the kitten heels we both bought last summer – with gold tips and...' I pause as some things just require dramatic effect, '...buckles.'

Lisa gasps and bites her fist. I savour the look of shock on her face and simply nod in vindication.

'O.M.G. buckles? Really?!'

I cock my head to the side and put my finger up, 'Did I mention the Cuban heel?'

Lisa holds her hands up in the air. 'Enough said! You absolutely did the right thing getting out of there. Surely it's a crime to even *sell* shoes like that! I mean men's white shoes unless they are designer plimsolls are a no-no in most parts of the capital, but to add buckles!' We both give a little shudder at the thought – now she understands.

'But, Gina even though this time you were totally justified to fly out of there as fast as your Carvela's could carry you – what about all the other times? They didn't all commit this cardinal sin and they *still* didn't get a second chance. I would go so far as to say that you didn't really even give them a first chance.'

Our mutual understanding was short-lived. Lisa is looking at me through narrowed eyes again. And again it's totally unjustified.

So, I'm 35 and still single. There are many of us females flying the flag of Singledom out there. This should be a time of solidarity, not suspicion. So what if people are always surprised to hear I'm not with anyone?

Just because I've received the odd wolf whistle, I mean what woman hasn't? To be honest, who really knows why men wolf whistle? I mean it could be part of an initiation into the construction industry for all we know – like drinking 100 tequila shots to be part of a fraternity or something..

Every woman should have standards, right? And I am simply a woman with standards that I'm in no rush to compromise that's all – even though I am now in my mid-thirties so admittedly I could hardly be accused of rushing.

I've been lucky enough to have a face that my Mum says "doesn't look like the back of a bus", but who wants to be sought after just for their looks anyway? I am the sum of more than just my shiny hair, high cheekbones and button nose which incidentally gets really red in winter. In fact, I could easily pass for Rudolph's cousin at Christmas and what girl would want to go out on dates in winter with the prospect of a reindeer like nose? Besides, doesn't every girl deserve to be loved for what's on the inside rather than the outside? Isn't what's in the mind more important than what's on the head? (Even if it is a rather overpriced haircut that I didn't know would cost that much until my hairdresser told me. You know it's just awkward to ask the price beforehand.)

I feel like I need a box to stand on right now in the middle of a big busy shopping square, waving a placard about a woman's right *not* to date.

'Gina? Admit it. The others weren't all *that* bad were they?'

I'm actually quite stunned right now. How can that thought enter her head, never mind pass her lips? I have valid non-fussy reasons for every guy with whom I did not continue a romantic liaison with. Every. Single. One.

'I mean what was wrong with Marko? He was a hunky Italian specimen of maleness if ever I saw one and he positively doted on you!'

'Hmph, he may have been an Italian stud but he wore bellbottoms. I mean, who wears bellbottoms in this day and age? And tartan ones at that. Do they even sell tartan in Italy?'

'Okay, what about Frederick? He was super smart.'

'And super boring. Even the lettuce wilted from his conversation.'

'Justin? He was really stylish – what was wrong there?'

'Justin was *too* stylish to be straight. He is a gay man-in-waiting who that closet is not going to be able to contain for much longer. Even *you* commented on his French manicure and the chandeliers he'd bought for his flat when we went to his house-warming party

'Okay, okay – you might have had a point about Justin. How about Steve? Wasn't he a journalist? He knew everything that was going on in the celebrity world. He must have had loads of interesting things to talk about.'

'Oh, he did. And the more he spoke, the more he lisped and the more he sprayed. I don't think I ever got rid of that bit of spinach that sailed out of his mouth onto my favourite white work shirt when he tried to say "exponentially". In fact, he was another Harold, only older and without the horrific shoes.

'Ronald? Martin? Norman?'

'Ronald – too short. He came up to my boobs when I had my flats on and liked the fact a little too much for my liking. Martin – too loud. My clip-ons kept falling off from the vibrations of his bellowing laugh. And Norman – too gassy.'

Lisa cringes her face 'Gassy, like you mean…?'

I nod 'Yes. It was like sitting next to a wind machine. And I'm not talking about the kind Beyoncé uses either.'

Lisa shakes her head at me.

'I just don't want you to end up alone'

'Honestly Lisa, I'm fine. I just don't want to have to kiss lots of frogs before I find my prince. And at least I'm still friends with them all.'

'Well, that's something I guess, but how many male friends does a girl need? Anyone would think collecting male friends was your hobby, you have so many.'

Lisa laughs and I laugh along with her hoping she doesn't notice mine has suddenly gone up an octave or two. I think it's time to break up this line of questioning before we start going too deep. Lying to my best friend is not something I'm good at so best not risk straying into conversational territory that I'd sooner stay out of.

'You wouldn't say that if they were your friends. Justin for instance – go shopping with him and it's like having your own personal stylist. He just has the eye. That jacket you saw me in two months ago that you borrowed and *still* haven't given back?'

Lisa blushes while still trying to look innocent, and that's no easy feat, 'Justin.' I finish.

'No way! He chose that for you?' Lisa sits bolt upright in the chair.

'Yes. He did a catwalk in it at the shop. All the customers started clapping, two asked him for his autograph and the resident stylist asked him to model three other jackets to help her hit her sales target. Oh, and did I mention that we got 25% off too?'

I can't help the smug look on my face. I just can't help it. Lisa slumps back in her seat, in surprise. Both waiters arrive back at the same time jostling one another as they try to put the peppermint tea and apple pie on the same spot in front of me. Lisa promptly takes the plate with the apple pie and shoos the waiters away. I smile my thanks and both waiters look dreamy-eyed as they link arms and walk off together. I take a quick sip and continue.

'...Frederick sorted out some accounting errors for the End of Year reports at the shop. Marko picked me up a couple of days ago in the pouring rain when I lost my Oyster card...'

'Okay, okay! I get it. Having lots of friends has its advantages.'

'It sure does. And all it costs is a home-cooked meal which I happily oblige with recipes from that Ultimate Chef cook book you bought me for my birthday last year.' There. That should put the lid on *that* subject. Yet, Lisa is still looking at me like she wants to ask me something more. My palms are getting a little sweaty. What if she asks me...no, she wouldn't even think to. No one would think to. And if by some strange twist of fate, she *did* think to, today is not the day for revelations. Especially one like mine.

'But Gina, don't you *want* to meet someone special?'

I laugh a little nervously and hope she doesn't notice, 'Duh Lisa, I meet people all the time.'

'Someone special, Gina. Don't you want to meet that someone who could be more than just a friend?'

Okay, I need to answer this question carefully. Very carefully indeed. I knew I should have watched that program about the 'Art of Deception' last night rather than WestEnders. Then again, Margie told her neighbour Beryl that she was pregnant with her husband's baby so missing that episode wasn't really an option.

'Of course I do.'

'Well, how are you going to know they can be that special someone when you won't allow them to get past the first date?'

I have my reasons, but as much as I love my best friend, she wouldn't understand and that's why I can't tell her.

'Lisa, I remember you blowing off that Archie fella because he had waist length hair. How is that any different to me?' I take a sip of my tea – it's getting cold but if I don't hold the cup; my fidgety fingers will give away how nervous I am about this line of conversation. 'Hey Lisa, did you watch WestEnders last night? Beryl's husband told Margie that she was nothing but a home wrecker and the baby wasn't his! Then Margie said...'

'Oh no, you don't Gina. No trying to change the subject! That's not happening today. What's going on? What aren't you telling me?'

'Geez Lisa, you're starting to sound like my mother!' I laugh nervously.

'I'm serious. Is there some reason why you don't want to meet someone? I don't know a single guy who wouldn't give his right arm for an evening in your company, or an attached guy for that matter who wouldn't have to think twice about ditching the partner they have for a chance of a date with you. You are the epitome of someone who could have any guy they wanted – literally.' Out of the corner of my eye I can see the two waiters looking our way and nodding vigorously as they serve the table next to ours.

'... so why don't you want one?' Lisa looks genuinely perplexed.

Meanwhile, I can't even think straight. She has asked the one question that I don't have a pre-prepared answer for. I don't want to lie to my best friend but at the same time, I would rather walk barefoot over hot coals than tell her the true reason why I don't have a boyfriend.

'Of course I want one, tch. Who wants to be alone forever?' What else could I say to buy myself more time to think of something better to say?

'Prove it.'

'What do you mean prove it?'

'I'm going to find you a fella. And every single guy I find you over the next couple of months, you have to promise to go on a full dinner date with. You are not allowed to find superficial fault with them and not allowed to throw them the "Let's be Friends" line.'

My jaw drops. Where did this suddenly come from? Why do I feel like I've been set up?

'...and provided nothing new comes up that isn't discovered in my background check or them wearing white pointy patent gold-tipped shoes with buckles...in fact, make that *any* shoes with buckles – if they want a second date with you, you have to say yes!'

I want to say no freaking way with every fibre of my being, but then she'd definitely suspect something was up and ask me straight out. Then I'd be forced to tell her the secret I've been holding out on her forever. We've told each other more or less everything since we were eleven. She's gonna be so mad at me. But worse than that, she's going to be so hurt that I didn't tell her. That I *couldn't* tell her. And I'd rather go on a few silly dates if it means my skeletons can stay safely in the closet.

'Fine. You're on. In fact, thank you for caring.'

I don't even know why I'm worrying. Most of Lisa's male friends are either taken, or taken with several females at the same time so there'd be no chance she'd want me entangled with any of them.

'And as most of my male friends are already involved or busy juggling between several women, my pool of potentials is quite small. That's why I'm going to enlist the help of a few other people who'll be more than happy to see you finally hooked up'

My ears prick up at this unexpected addendum. Ask whom to help exactly?

Three

'Now, I knew it would have to be people that know you and the type of guy that would suit you,' Lisa leans forward in her seat again, barely able to contain her excitement, 'I spoke to your Mum and Dad first and foremost – obviously. Actually, your Mum already had someone in mind.'

'Oh, she did, did she?' My sarcasm bounces off Lisa into the ether as she continues with her Help List.

'Your Grandma and Cousin Mona...mmm... Patsy your assistant – I figured she was bound to see a few single guys buying sexy underwear for their Mum's on Mother's Day.' Really? That's really who she thinks single guys are buying sexy lingerie for? Eew!

'Mr Shah from the corner shop. Oh! And you'll never believe who else has offered to help you?'

To be honest, I actually can't believe any of this. '...Delilah!'

My eyes open even wider than I thought possible at the sound of *that* name. Lisa beckons to the waiter to bring another slice of Apple pie.

'All of the above have kindly pitched in their support. Actually, everyone was quite eager to help. Between us, we should be able to get you enough dates in the next eight weeks to have you engaged by Christmas!' Lisa is clapping her hands, whilst I just want to take mine and wrap them around my own neck! Family, so-called Friends and Foe – that being my arch enemy Delilah Pine. This is who she has roped in to help me find a man that I didn't ask for! Clearly this is something Lisa has been scheming for a while and I've walked straight into her plot. How did I not spot this? I can see her mind still ticking over.

'I reckon we'll be able to get the ball rolling on Project DateLock straight away.' This is a project? And it has a name? I'm speechless! It's my turn to beckon to the waiter now – I need something a whole lot stronger than peppermint tea.

'I'm quite sure there'll be no shortage of guys wanting to take you out. Actually, I should add the two waiters here to the list too. At this rate, we probably won't even need eight weeks.' Lisa is tucking into her second slice of apple pie with gusto while both waiters are jostling one another to get to the table first to take my alcohol order. Maybe there is an employee of the day award for who serves the most customers? Lisa seems really confident about getting into this. More confident than I feel in getting out of it.

I sit silently while she continues telling me how she went about selecting her partners in crime. I sip the glass of wine that Waiter Two brought back in record time with a triumphant smile on his face. Lisa has finally paused for breath – the excitement at having this opportunity to manage my lack of love-life clearly evident. Project Management was always her strong suit. Never did I dream that I would be one of the projects

'Fine. I'll leave this matter in your capable hands then.' I give a wide smile and hope that the stem of the glass doesn't snap from how tightly I'm holding it. 'Oh, look at the time, Lisa. Got to dash back to the shop, I'm expecting a delivery. Speak to you later'

I drain the last remnants of the wine in one gulp, jump up and kiss my so-called pal on the cheek before flying out of the restaurant in a semi-panic, but not before both waiters have rushed over to me, one giving me a takeaway menu and the other a 20% off next visit voucher. I glance over my shoulder to wave goodbye to Lisa, only to see her talking to a third waiter who is shaking his head at the other two and pointing to himself as Lisa jots down notes on a napkin.

I've got to think clearly about this. I mean, it's not like I've not been in this match-making situation before. In my twenties, I was subjected to many a match-making attempt – in fact, as far as my mother was concerned, if he was alive then he was potential son-in-law material. Now I think about it, I'm sure there was an on-going bet on my road as to when I'd get a boyfriend. I wouldn't be surprised if that bet was still running.

Geez, why is everyone around me still so eager to get me hitched anyhow? I can just imagine it must have been neck and neck between my Gran and Mr Shah to see who could set me up first. Gran, because she thinks I'm too fussy and wants some grandbabies and Mr Shah, simply because he has a *lot* of cousins.

If my situation were not...shall we say, as it is - I wouldn't even mind the help. It would be like being the only client in an exclusive dating agency. But my situation is as it is - so this is the worst thing ever that could have happened to me. Well, the second worst *because* of the first worst – which is obviously my situation. And what's more, I can't just politely refuse these dates. I have no choice but to go along with this or Lisa will suspect something and start questioning me and then...no. I don't want to think about where that road leads right now. Whatever happens, I'll just have to make sure that these guys won't *want* to ask me out again. And that unfortunately might be a bit of a challenge.

To explain a bit more - I won a few Beauty pageants back in the day...all twenty-three that my Mum entered me into behind my back. I wanted to pull out every time because who really wants the boys they went to Uni with seeing them in their underwear? But Mum's eyes would well up whenever I protested, guilting me into changing my mind with some reason or other like she always wanted compete herself but couldn't because she had me, or she married Dad, or she missed the train to Brighton! (I never worked out how that was relevant either) – in any case, she knows tears are my downfall, ever since she bawled her eyes out hard when I played Mary in my first Christmas Nativity play when I was five. All the parents stared at her and all the kids on the stage who knew she was my Mum (because she kept sobbing 'That Mary's my baby!') stared at me. Let's just say I learned at a very young age that I don't do embarrassment very well and Mum's tears are forever a reminder of that.

To be honest though, the pageant experiences weren't all bad – all the prize money I won mostly paid the deposit for the premises of my luxury underwear shop - The Art of Lingerie. I even wore some of my lingerie designs in a few of the shows so that was good free publicity. The competitions stopped after Dad punched out one of his workmates. He caught him simulating over one of my winning pictures that was in a promotional calendar in a way that no father wants to see a workmate simulating over a picture of their daughter.

Anyway, that's the reason why nearly everyone around me thinks I should be with someone – because as my Gran always says,

'There is no reason why a Beauty pageant winner shouldn't be married.'

What never crosses her mind is that what might be a beauty queen to one Gran, might be just some female who likes to walk across a public stage in her underwear with a dodgy gold plated crown on her head, to another. And the other side of the coin that seems to cross everyone else's mind is the fact that as I'm not married *or* in a relationship *or* serial dating and half way through my thirties, must therefore mean I'm too fussy or a snob.

If only it *was* one of those reasons. I wouldn't feel so embarrassed and wish the ground would swallow me up if it was one of *those* reasons. Plus, no-one would believe the real reason anyway, not in a million years.

And now my best friend wants to put me in a situation I've avidly avoided for goodness knows how long with goodness knows how many guys. That cann*ot* happen.

So I need a plan. Well, two plans really.

Plan A - I have to try and get to everyone she's roped into this crazy scheme of hers and convince them that I can meet the right guy without their help.

Or Plan B, I'll just have to go on those arranged dates. But by the end of those dates, I'll make sure those guys wished they never got a taste of this arm candy.

Four

I don't go back to the shop like I told Lisa. I did intend to - there actually really *is* a delivery today, but Patsy my assistant can take care of that. Instead, I browse around the shops for a few hours – shopping really is a type of therapy. I don't find anything suitable enough to curb my sudden anxiety so I jump on the 247 bus just pulling into the bus stop and head towards home. The driver looks familiar but as I can't place the face I just flash my bus pass at him and sit down. All I want to do now is go home and think. A hot bath to clear my mind is what I need right now. Maybe I'll add one of those Bubble bath balls that Gran bought me for Christmas. My head is all over the place with this Date-or-die plan I suddenly find myself embroiled in. I need to focus if I'm going to sabotage the plan and still keep my secret intact.

As I see my stop approaching, I decide to take the shortcut through the park. I've been so wrapped up in my thoughts, I didn't even realise what a lovely day it is. The sun is flooding through the trees. The park is quite busy today with people walking their dogs on retractable leashes and kids messing about after school when they should be on their way home.

I suddenly see a football flying towards my head like a Quidditch bludger, and I only just manage to duck in time to see it smack into a tree then fall onto Benji, an annoying Yorkshire Terrier that lives two doors away and yaps non-stop every evening until 10.00pm when he's suddenly mysteriously silent. Oh dear...he does look a little dazed, but at least he's stopped yapping. Hopefully that will last until tonight.

'Oh m-m-my gosh! I'm so so-so-sorry Gina; I meant to kick it towards my mu-mum and it j-just...'

'Hey Danny, no harm no foul.' I walk over to the tree to get the ball – the terrier is just regaining consciousness and yapping what appears to be double time now. I pretend to do some fancy footwork with the ball in my 4 inch heels before kicking it back towards him. Danny Matthews is my twelve-year-old next door neighbour. He is adorably sweet and has this strange part-time stutter. I watch as the ball rolls past him and he stands there just staring at me.

'Ahem, Danny? There's your ball...' He shakes his head as if coming out of a trance.

'Th-th-thanks G-gina. Me and Mu-Mum were just having a k-kick about. W-want to j-join us?'

Mrs Matthews is bobbing up and down impatiently 'Come on Danny! What's the hold up? Hi Gina', she gives me a wave.

'Gee Mum, I'm coming! I nearly knocked Gina out with the ball so I'm just making sure she's okay' Danny rolls his eyes at his mum.

I think it's great the way his stutter goes away when he talks to his Mum.

'Hey Tommy,' he then shouts over to a school friend 'make sure you don't forget the science notes for school tomorrow. Or you are so gonna be in detention again!'

And when he talks to his friends.

'I hope you're okay too Benji, that was a hard rebound you took just now from my football'

And when he talks to little yapping dogs.

'So-so-sorry again, G-gina'

'As I said Danny, no problem.' I wave back to Mrs Matthews and give Danny a little wink. All this running up and down has given him a healthy flush to his cheeks...in fact, his whole face.

I begin walking again and start to squint. Not that I need glasses or anything, I just tend to squint when I see something odd. Like my mother walking towards my house when she's supposed to be at Westfield Shopping centre. And surely that isn't Gran pulling up in a taxi outside my front door? She's supposed to be running a Bingo tournament today. What's going on? What are they doing here?

I cross the road to get a bit closer to my house – and see Dad's car in the drive. Okay, something fishy is definitely going on. If they are all at my house, then it can only be for one reason. Darn that Lisa, she's as fast as the Flash! It hasn't even been a couple of hours since she told me about this dating plan. Only she could have gathered everyone together already – and to add insult to injury, at my house of all places. This is all happening too fast. I'm not prepared; I'm not even dressed for it. If I'm going to be relaxed and on form to foil their plans, it should at least be in my bunny slippers. I need to think...I need more time...I need...Skittles. Yes, that sugary sweetness always helps me focus.

I take a detour to Mr Shah's corner shop. I reach the store just as he's changing the door sign to CLOSED. I quicken my pace to a kind of walk-run and manage to shove the door open before he gets a chance to turn the lock.

'Ooh, just in time!' I say brightly. 'Isn't it a little early to be closing up shop?' I peer around some shelves suspiciously.

'I am on the way to meeting at your house. I am thinking you should be there and not here?'

Okay, I knew she shanghaied Mr Shah into her plan, but knowing and *knowing* - well, it's just two completely different things isn't it.

'Yes, I am indeed on my way home right now. Just popped in for some...for some...' My mind goes uncharacteristically blank of everything but Lisa's grinning face. Mr Shah waves the biggest packet of Skittles in front of me

'I order them special for you as I know they are your favourites. I was to be bringing them to your house, but you can have them now. Your friend Lisa says to not being late so I am locking up now. See you in a short while.'

'Thanks, Mr Shah. I'm just going to make a quick phone call. See you in a few minutes.'

I spin on my heel, and walk in the opposite direction to my house. I take the empty seat at the bus stop and hold my chin in thought. Lisa has clearly moved quickly on this to stop me from getting to everyone first. In a matter of minutes, I'm going to be face to face with all her accomplices. Well, that's Plan A out the window. Lisa is at this very minute speeching everyone on what a wonderful thing they're doing for me, and that I desperately need their help, blah de blah de blah. Going in now and trying to tell them otherwise will just add fuel to Lisa's fire when what I need to do is douse it.

So. Looks like Plan B it is then.

Five

I walk back towards the house with my plan in mind. As I approach, I dart behind a tree, crouch down and crawl over to the window. As I peep through...damn, my heel is getting tangled and now I've ripped my tights. Bloomin' overgrown weeds. Mental note - buy some shears in the Argos sale. I attempt to peep again and get an eyeful of the chosen panel Lisa has assembled to help her get me a date.

I can hear her voice in my head.

'...Mr Shah just knows so many people, and he's already been trying to hook you up for years.'

Naturally, no matchmaking plan would be complete without the assistance of Mr Shah. Not only does he know the world, but he owns most of the high street – which is probably why he knows the whole world. As well as the corner shop and the coffee shop that he's just opened where the old Woolworths used to be, he also owns the local post office, laundrette and supermarket. He also co-owns the dry cleaners as I previously mentioned with Michel – and I'm sure that only happened because Michel got engaged to his daughter last year and he doesn't trust him to run the business on his own. Now I think about it, I'm sure he also mentioned buying a KFC franchise that will sell halal fried chicken.

Of course, I know that the key reason for inveigling Mr Shah into her plot is that he has a *big* family. Huge in fact. I'm sure he's related to half of India as he's been introducing me to a different cousin every time I pop into the corner shop for a Kitkat for years. An endless gene pool of potential candidates. He's standing over by the window, probably to keep an eye out for the advert that he's just arranged to go on the side of the number 247 bus. It wasn't on the one I travelled on so it can't have gone past yet.

Gran is sitting on the armrest – she says it's too much trouble to pull herself up from the middle of my super-slouchy sofa.

'...and your Gran has got great taste in guys, so there'll be no getting out of a second date with who she finds...'

And of course, she's right. My Gran just has an eye for matchmaking. She's set up eight couples already in the past year, three are getting engaged, one is planning a cruise around the Caribbean and two have just moved in together. And they're just from where she plays Bingo. She could stand in for Cupid if he ever needed a day off.

Mum is sitting next to her sipping a cup of tea and waving at something on TV.

'...your Mum actually already had someone in mind...'

Surprise, surprise. My Mum thinks my biological clock is tolling (which is much louder than ticking) and hands out business cards with my details on to single males at every opportunity.

I can't really blame her since she's never seen her only daughter with a significant other. Even so, it's not really the done thing asking Jim who delivers the internet shopping from Tesco (who, by the way, is nearly 70 and barely manages to get the shopping bags to the door without wheezing) if he wants to date your daughter.

And as for promising me to my 12-year-old neighbour Danny because she overheard him tell a friend without stuttering that he thought I was the prettiest woman he'd ever seen - well, let's not even go there. It's one reason of many that have made me question to this very day what I was thinking when I decided to buy a house opposite where my parents live. And then I remember that I can pop in for Mum's melt-in-the-mouth pastries at any time and then I remember exactly what I was thinking.

The Not-so-delightful-Delilah is at the edge of the sofa painting her nails with ruby red nail varnish – just the shade you'd expect a witch to wear.

'...Delilah said she will be more than happy to help find you a date or two if it'll help you get over Paul. Although, I think it's more to stop the not so subtle drooling he directs at you every time he sees you. In any case, she is on board!'

Delilah Pine is not a friend. She lives opposite me, next door to Mum and Dad. She hates me because her boyfriend Paul who she's been with for five years dated me first for about two weeks when I was about nine years old. I mean do dates when you're nine even count as real dates? Plus, Delusional Delilah didn't even live in the area back then but she seems to think it's given me one up on her. Now it's her mission to even some imaginary score.

She comes to every function on the road with Paul wrapped around her waist like a belt just to gloat at how wonderful their relationship is and to highlight my lack of one. Delilah epitomises everything about the saying of keeping your enemies close. If she's been wangled in to help here, that means Lisa means business about finding me a boyfriend – and breathing is the basic criteria. I am sure that will be the only compatibility Delilah will be looking for if she's looking for someone for me.

Cousin Mona is talking on her smart phone as usual by the doorway.

'...Your cousin Mona said she might know a few potentials.'

Of course Cousin Mona would be pulled into this. She's a student at Milltown University and will definitely be utilised to scope out any eligible lecturers and probably even any single students. Lisa's made it clear that there is a timetable at play here so any and all possibilities will likely be considered no matter how ludicrous I may think they are.

'...Patsy has already said she'll keep an eye out for any dishy date-to-be's that happen to pass through the shop...'

Hah, lucky for me I'd scheduled Patsy to work at the shop all day today. Well, Patsy dearest, I'll just have to make sure you're so busy; you won't have time to keep your head up, never mind your eyes out.

Dad is sitting next to Mum in the middle of the sofa, leafing through a newspaper...no, actually, that's my latest edition 'Style and Home' magazine which I haven't even read yet.

'...your Dad...well your Dad can be an observer.'

My Dad doesn't think anyone is good enough for me. Never thought I'd see the day when that was a good thing. He's probably only really here because Mum has dragged him along. At least that's one ally I have in my corner.

And, then there's the instigator herself – Lisa. She's pacing up and down in front of the TV. She's holding a clipboard as she paces and is chewing on a pencil deep in thought. I don't need three guesses to know what she's thinking about either. She's so proud of her sneaky plan. And I have no choice but to go along with it if I don't want to jeopardise revealing my secret.

Shit! Mr Shah is walking towards the front door – he mustn't see me spying on my own house! I turn to duck behind the bin, and the darned overgrown weed strikes again! My foot gets tangled and over I go! Off comes the bin lid, over goes the bin and out comes the rubbish – all over me!

I close my eyes in silent prayer that Mr Shah didn't notice. I hold my breath - and my nose. This is some pongy rubbish, what on earth do I eat? Mr Shah rings the doorbell...I don't think he's seen me - I literally have been saved by the bell.

I open my eyes in relief and smile – a smile which is suddenly frozen in place as I see my whole family crammed at the window, all craning to see the commotion that is me.

'Hi' I squeak

Lisa gives me a strange look. 'Hi...back at you?'

'I...erm...was looking for...erm...it, and I tripped and...well... as you can see!' I flourish my hands and give a nervous laugh. 'So. Can somebody give me a little assistance please?'

Dad reaches over and grabs my hands, held by my Mum at the belt of his pants to make sure he doesn't get unbalanced.

'Gina! Are you okay love?' Mum's looking at me rather oddly, and clearly looking for more than a yes or no answer. As is everyone else, who are just staring at me questioningly. To buy myself some time, I make a play of brushing the week's contents from my bin off my clothes and smoothing back my hair from my eyes. I don't even know what I'm going to say, but the first step is to open my mouth, right? So I open my mouth...and the doorbell rings and the knocker knocks and all we can hear is...

'Hello? Hello? It's Mr Shah?'

I'd forgotten he was at the front door!

'I'll let him in!' I hold up my front door keys and give them a jingle. Before anyone can question me further, I dart around to where Mr Shah is who has just noticed me covered in trash.

'Don't ask.' I say as I shove my key into the door and then shove Mr Shah straight into Mum who must have come to open the door. I use this moment of distraction to run upstairs.

'Just going to freshen up out of these rubbish-sodden clothes - won't be a minute!' I run to my bedroom and slam the door quickly. What am I going to do? What am I going to say? I lean my head against the door. I'm starting to hyperventilate. Where is a paper bag when you need it? Ugh...stuck on the bottom of my shoe! As I turn to lean my back against the door and remove the paper, I see Lisa sitting on my bed still chewing that pencil and looking straight at me.

'Phew! Who'd have thought running up a flight of stairs could make someone so out of breath!' I take a few more deep breaths and fan my face for further effect. I give Lisa a big smile.

'Hmm...are you *sure* you're okay with this date thing, Gina?'

Double damn my best friend for knowing me so well! But as much as I want to scream 'NOOOOOOO!' that would lead to more questions which would lead to divulging my secret which I'm not ready to do any time soon.

'Of *course* I am! My friends and family – and even someone who hates my guts - are trying to find me the perfect someone. Who wouldn't be okay with that?'

I walk over to my wardrobe and pull out a purple satin dress with a flourish, 'look I'm even dressing for the occasion.' Actually, maybe not this dress, I remember now why it was strategically placed in the back of my wardrobe. I throw it in the corner and continue touching hangers for effect.

'I didn't tell you about this first meeting because I wanted you to get used to the idea.' Oh, but go ahead and use my house to entrap me why don't you. Never thought giving my best friend my spare key would come back to bite me in the rear end. I give her a sickly sweet smile.

'Sure, I get it.'

'You said you had to rush off for a delivery? Didn't it come?

'Huh?'

'It's just that you got back here kind of quickly considering you left from the coffee shop to go to your Lingerie shop to sort out a delivery and now you're here.'

'Right! Yes...the delivery...aah yes, I remembered Patsy was due to come in when I nearly got to the shop so it didn't make sense to come all the way back to meet you again. It was a nice afternoon so thought why not spend some of it in the garden.' I add a little high pitched laugh at the end and already, I'm regretting it and praying that it hasn't oversold my excuse.

Lisa looks at me hard for a few more seconds and then breaks out into a smile. 'Great!'

She jumps up from the bed with zest and starts to help me go through my wardrobe.

'I've already thought about working out a timetable for you, so figured why not gather everyone and get started right away.' she continues as she holds up my white silk blouse against herself.

'But, Gina...?' Lisa suddenly looks serious, 'I don't know if we'll be able to find you a perfect guy...'

Before I can say "Lets call the whole thing off then because every girl wants Mr Perfect", she suddenly perks up again

'...but we should definitely be able to find a good guy for you. I've got a really good vibe about this. See you downstairs in a mo!'

She shoves the white silk blouse into my hands with a thumbs-up and skips through the door like an energetic puppy while I feel like I want to collapse in a pile on the floor next to the purple satin dress. I drag my heels towards the shower.

My whole family is downstairs with my best friend, my mortal enemy and the local business mogul – all eager to put me in a situation within eight weeks what I've avidly avoided for all of my adult life. I've got to stay strong. I roll my hand into a fist and punch my chest twice – cough, cough – perhaps a little too hard. It always seems more playful than painful when they do it on TV. Anyway, thinking of what's at stake here gives me new resolve. I'll just have to play this meeting by ear.

Six

With battle armour of Levi Jeans, Lisa-chosen white silk blouse and pink bunny slippers, I creep downstairs and peek over the banister. I smooth down my hair self-consciously – there wasn't a lot I could do with it in ten minutes – a brush alone simply wasn't getting out lasagne leftovers and three-day old melted cheese. I see a strategic re-shuffle has taken place and there is now a gaping gap in the middle of the sofa where Dad was previously sitting. I don't need three guesses to know that gaping space has been created for me. The courage I had built up pre-shower deserts me and I turn to creep back upstairs. Before I can even do a partial 180-degree turnaround, I hear Lisa's dulcet tones.

'Ah, Gina! There you are! We were beginning to think you'd been sucked down the plughole. Let's get this party started.'

I take a few deep breaths, roll my head around and flex my arms outwards before completing the flight of stairs and strolling into the room with a confidence I'm far from feeling. I muster up a big smile.

'Good afternoon everyone' I deliberately aim for the armchair by the window.

'Over here dear, come and sit by me' Mum pats the empty cushion between her and Dad with an innocent look. I turn to Lisa; her eyes share the same innocence which confirms my thoughts that this seating arrangement has indeed been pre-orchestrated. I change direction and lower myself between Mum and Dad. Dad pats my knee absently and turns the page to now read an article called Fifty Shades Off White – from Cream to Beige. Lisa gives a little cough to get everyone's attention

'Okay, everybody. Thanks for coming here today on such short notice. I know some of you are really busy and would usually need more than a fortnight to make arrangements so you being here today for Gina is really appreciated'

A fortnight? So this was planned...two WEEKS ago?

'So I'll get right down to business. Basically, our aim here is to help our beloved friend and family member...'

Delilah aggressively filing her nails, gives a snort, which Lisa in true friend-fashion completely ignores and continues as if no snort occurred, '...Gina to find a decent guy.'

'...more like any guy.' Delilah adlibs in what was definitely too loud to be a whisper. Lisa ignores her again and continues,

'...because as we know there are many guys who already have girlfriends that nevertheless are still lusting after our girl...' Lisa pauses and looks sideways at Delilah who has gone slightly pink but says nothing and continues to file her nails, a little less aggressively now. I smile to myself and give my friend a silent hi-five. Please note Lisa's hi-five is for shutting up Cow-face Delilah, not for arranging this debacle.

'...and we know she deserves to have an available guy lusting after her instead. As that deserving stranger is taking mysteriously too long to find, we are going to help her. Lord knows why she needs the help as she has got to be one of the most beautiful, sexy...I mean seriously, what is *wrong* with these guys if they can't...'

'Lisa, I'm sure we can all see how...palatable Gina's features are – so if we could get back to the point of this meeting?' Delilah has found her tongue again I see. This time though, I agree with her. I want Lisa to just get on with this.

'Yes, Lisa – how is this going to work, exactly?' I can't believe I'm even asking the question.

'Well, we set the dates up for you – and you go on them'.

Sounds simple enough, but things are never simply simple if Lisa's got anything to do with it.

'We are going to pool our resources to help you find Mr Right. You know the old saying – too many cooks make Sunday dinner quicker.'

I can't remember exactly how that old saying goes, but I'm pretty sure it was about spoiling some sort of soup.

Mum is beaming and claps her hands in glee. 'Ooh, I'm so excited about helping my little rose-bud.'

'So, what I'd like each of you to do, is put forward your candidate – tell us a little bit about them. I'll take notes so that I can do some background work,'

Really? She can get background information on people? Why did I not know this when I wanted to get some dirt on that cow Sheila? I actually mean physical dirt – like what you pot plants with. Sheila has a dirt-phobia. Sheila deliberately-by-accident spilled hot coffee on me because Gerard who she's wanted to date forever, asked me out. How was that my fault? My revenge was going to be to drop some soil in her hair, but after that day she just disappeared – and now I find out Lisa could have found her. Tch.

'...then I can slot them into Gina's date diary. This way there'll be no double-bookings to ensure she can go out with each and every one of the eligible bachelors you put forward.' Lisa is chewing her pencil thoughtfully.

'Erm...you have a date diary for me?'

Lisa holds up her clipboard and taps it at me. And there was me thinking it was just to make her look official. Mr Shah walks away from the window over to Lisa, suddenly looking a little too interested in the contents on her clipboard for my liking.

'Lisa, I have many cousins visiting from India who would be happy to meet the lovely Gina. Five of them are single and looking for wives. In fact,

Cousin Naveen will be arriving tonight and would love to meet the lovely Gina.' Suddenly Mr Shah and Lisa's heads are siamesed together. They start whispering to each other as she writes notes and starts texting on her phone. She'd better be telling him that only women on chat shows like Jeremy Kyle go out with *five* members of the same family.

'Great, Mr Shah, let me know the availability of the others too and I'll slot them into Gina's date diary.'

'Erm...what about *my* availability? Not that I don't appreciate all of this, but unfortunately I'm quite busy with work for the next few weeks.'

I turn to Mr Shah 'You understand don't you, Mr Shah? That as a business owner if you don't dedicate time to nurture it and grow it and keep up with the trends, then before you know it competition will sneak in and steal away your customers with BOGOFs and LRs'

'Ooh I know BOGOF is buy one get one free but I just can't figure out the LR one.' Mum squeezes her eyes shut and clenches her fists together to try and work out the abbreviation.

'It's Loyalty Reward, Mum.' I sigh.

'That's it! That was on the tip of my tongue!' Mum practically jumps out of her seat pointing at me manically. Mr Shah I'm happy to see is slowly nodding in agreement. Good. If I can turn one against this crazy scheme, then it's only a matter of time before I turn the others.

'You're available Gina.' Lisa doesn't even look up from her clipboard.

'I'll have you know that my work appointments...'

'...are all in the morning.' Lisa finishes my sentence. 'I already checked your work schedule with your assistant Patsy. You've nothing major until the autumn sales start which isn't until a couple of months and we should have you sorted by then.'

I can hardly believe it. I have been sold out by the Judas I employ. I don't know how Jesus was so calm. I feel like I could cheerfully wring a certain someone's neck. I make a mental note that re-organising stock in the store room is going to be Patsy's number one chore on Friday. Especially as I saw a big old spider near the cotton specials.

'That is true, but unfortunately, that's only my *work* diary, I'm pretty sure that...'

'And your Gran told me that when she checked your personal diary there wasn't anything major going on in there either.'

I swirl round to Gran and put on my most shocked and indignant expression. My shock is actually genuine because there was a point when I truly thought about writing my secret down in the notes section of that same personal diary. Gran would have known, then everyone would have known and before you know it, I would have been suitable fodder for the Jeremy Kyle show after all. I say a silent prayer of thanks that I binned that idea!

'My *personal* Diary, Gran? Really?'

Gran flaps her hand dismissively at me as she goes over to Lisa and too starts looking at the clipboard 'Oh, Virginia. It was there for anyone to find - buried in the back of your wardrobe in a shoe box with shoes still in it, underneath that blue hat box with the hat you bought for Ascot three years ago, sandwiched between a few other shoe boxes and that sack of clothes you said you wanted to take to a car boot sale. If you'd really wanted to keep it a secret you'd have hidden it in your underwear drawer. No woman wants to go through another woman's underwear drawer.'

Am I alone in thinking that a woman shouldn't want to rummage through another woman's cast offs in the depths of her wardrobe either? Evidently I am because I look around to see Delilah blowing her nails dry and nodding along in agreement.

Cousin Mona is doing a 'Duh!' face as if to say who doesn't know that? Clearly, I missed the class where they taught about "How to hide your diary", but more importantly, I made sure I caught the one about "How to keep a secret" and that's going to be a hell of a lot harder for them to find out, than what I'm doing next Friday.

'So does anyone have any more ideas as to how we can maximise dates for Gina?' Lisa holds up her pen to command attention.

'We could have an auction and the prize could be a date with Gina.' Cousin Mona has finished her phone conversation and now appears to be texting someone as she offers her suggestion.

'Remember all those guys at Gran's Bingo Christmas Party who were fighting over the last piece of mistletoe when Gina walked in? Limp haired Leslie ended up with a black eye, and Toby who stacks shelves at Mr Shah's supermarket fractured his toe. I reckon they'd all bid. Plus, an auction would definitely be a less painful way for them to meet Gina.'

'Good idea!' Lisa is writing quite quickly now.

'Ooh, yes! And I could make some pies for a picnic basket that they could take on their prize date...' Mum claps her hands again.

'*Great* idea, Mrs Robbins! Keep them coming people.' Lisa is scribbling furiously.

'Yes, I quite agree' Delilah blows gently on her just polished nails

'Then we can give whatever monies raised to a good cause. Like Gina's hairdresser.'

Oh, whatever. Like she's never caught her shoe heel in weeds and landed headfirst in a bin full of rubbish.

Lisa's pencil is going to combust into flames if it whizzes across the clipboard any faster. So much for shutting this idea down before it starts. It's time I put my two pence worth in.

'Really, everyone - this is becoming...'

'...we could slot that auction idea in between here and here, what do you think?' Lisa is now surrounded by Mum, Gran and Mr Shah who seems to be pointing at possible free days that his numerous cousins could be slotted into. Delilah is smiling smugly to herself and Dad is now reading another article – Top European cities for bed bug infestations. It's like I'm not even here. I clamp my hands over my eyes and count to ten. When

I remove my hands this is all going to be just a bad dream. I count to twenty instead and when I remove my hands, it looks like nearly everyone is now hovering around Lisa and her clipboard all trying to slot their suggestions into the date diary and all talking at the same time about...age limits?

'Anyone under 25 might be a little too young to want to settle down. 12-year-old Danny is a lovely young man, but it'll take far too long before he's legal and Gina doesn't have that kind of time.' Mum is tapping her chin thoughtfully.

'And over 60 should be out of bounds too because then we'll be dipping into my pool and there aren't many suitors in there as it is.'

Gran taps the clip board and Lisa seems to reluctantly nod and scribble something out.

Delilah has now joined them and points to the clipboard with her nail file '...if she wears yellow, I read somewhere that it's good luck...'

That cow knows I hate yellow – it makes me look like a bottle of mustard. I slump back against the seat and realise Dad is the only one not joining in the furore. Probably because he's still engrossed in that magazine. I crane over his shoulder to see what he's so fixated on now – because bed bugs can't be that interesting. The title seems to loom out of the magazine in 3D - "How to screen a potential date". When I notice that he's also made notes in the margin, it hits me that I have no-one on my side in this. It truly is me against the living room. I pinch myself to make sure this isn't all just a bad dream

'Ouch!' I flinch at my own strength. Everyone goes silent and looks at me a little strangely for a few seconds before shrugging their shoulders and resuming their plotting.

'Right everyone...' Lisa claps her hands, this time to get everyone's attention again. Everyone has now splintered off into little groups comparing each other's suggestions. This is really happening.

'I've quickly scanned Gina's date diary here and I can happily say she will be out at least once a week for the next couple of months'

Mr Shah raises his hand, but Lisa jumps in '...except for week three where she will be dating a succession of your cousins, Mr Shah, before they fly back to India, I've made a note. And of course, tomorrow which we've set up for your Cousin Naveen.' Mr Shah lowers his hand and nods.

'So everyone, I will text you all with details of the next meeting...'

'Erm...hold up. You've arranged a date for me, for tomorrow?'

'Yeah, thought I'd give you some time – he wanted to meet tonight and I was like hello? Give the girl a chance to put on some lip gloss already.' Lisa shakes her head in disbelief, then looks up at me suspiciously. 'Why? Is there a problem with tomorrow night? You're available, he's available, you said you were okay with what we're doing...unless you're *not* really okay with it and there's some secret reason you're not telling me?'

'No! Noooo. Of course there's no secret reason. Why would you say that? Why would you think that? What have you heard? Well, there's nothing to hear so...' Lisa is looking at me strangely – the way that someone looks at you when you start babbling. So I stop babbling abruptly and feign a look of absolute calmness 'I just wanted to know what time, that's all.'

Lisa gives me a long look and then breaks out into a big smile.

'It's tomorrow at 5.00p.m. That way, you can meet straight after work.'

'Great.' I say.

Well, at least this isn't a bad dream like I first thought. What this is, is a bad reality.

Seven

Mr Shah's Newsagent doesn't open until 7.00am.
It's 6.50am now but I want to be ready to burst
through the door when he opens up in ten minutes. He's naturally going to wonder why I'm up
so early seeing as the Art of Lingerie doesn't open
until 10.00am. My plan is to tell him I'm getting
a very early start doing stock taking so I need a
giant pack of Skittles to keep me and Patsy going
– then I can nonchalantly steer the conversation
into yesterday's proceedings. That sounds reasonable enough, doesn't it?

'Look, Mummy it's a princess!' A little girl
points in my direction as she walks past.

'It's not nice to point sweetheart' her mother
smiles at me apologetically.

I smile absently thinking there isn't anyone else
around at this time of the morning so it must be
her imaginary friend. I could do with an imagi-

nary friend right now. My mind is still in turmoil. I hardly got a wink of sleep last night worrying about this date. I may not be able to cancel meeting up with Cousin Naveen, but there's nothing in the rules to say that I can't manipulate Mr Shah into doing it whilst I browse through the various Skittle flavours on offer.

'Morning Gina, you are being here very early today, even before me!' Mr Shah is holding a bunch of keys that could rival a jailer.

'Stock taking – you know how it is Mr Shah. So, thought I'd get an early start and something sugary – in that order.' I give a laugh and hope it doesn't sound as high pitched to him as it does to me.

'I have just had some new sweets very much like your favourites. They are on the corner shelf.' Mr Shah pushes open the door to the sound of a tinkling bell and immediately starts busying himself with shop stuff whilst I'm still thinking about how to bring this date topic up un-suspiciously.

'Gina, did your mother tell you that I am speaking to My Cousin Naveen and he is telling me that he is trimming his moustache for your date and bought a new hair gel.'

He is so proud of his cousins. He's been telling Mum a fascinating fact about a different one for years –in fact, nearly every time she pops in for some eggs or a loaf of bread.'

'Yes, Mr Shah she did. About five minutes after you told her I believe. She also told me about the private online elocution lesson he took in case I couldn't understand his accent. She didn't even miss out the bit about the skinny jeans he decided not to wear because they were so tight they made him talk like a girl.'

'Ah yes, Cousin Naveen is looking very much forward to later. You are too, yes?'

'Of course I am...well, I should say I *was* looking forward to tonight...' Mr Shah is humming what sounds like a bhangra remix of 'Everybody in Love' by JLS. I give a big sigh for added effect.

'Yes,' I continue, 'tonight would have been great if only...'

'Something is wrong, Gina?'

'Well, I don't want to let anyone down but I think I ate something dodgy last night after the meeting and my stomach is still a bit tender. Not sure I'll be able to cope with anything other than crackers or dry toast today without running to the loo straight after – if you know what I mean...'

I taper off hoping that Mr Shah will fill in the blanks while I inspect a packet of peach and punch drops. Hmm...I might actually buy some of these.

'Oh dear, if you are feeling not well, the night will not be starting off very good. Would some Camomile tea help?'

'Hmm, that makes me sleepy'

'Peppermint?'

'Ooh, that gives me wind.'

'Honey and Lemon?'

'Just call me the Burp Queen if I even sip that!' I give a little laugh.

'Coconut water?'

'Allergic.' I shrug my shoulders

'Hot chocolate?'

'On a diet' I whisper. I have been revising all the possible variations, permutations, connotations and every other "tion" this conversation could come up with. And I am confident I have covered everything that could possibly be thrown at me to get out of this date. Mr Shah scratches his head in confusion and then shrugs his shoulders back at me.

'You are indeed a diamond girl, Gina Robbins' he says and then continues to stock the shelf. Okay...I clearly missed *this* variation. What does that even mean? I've given every excuse as to why my stomach ailment is practically incurable and why he should tell his Cousin and get the date cancelled, yet instead that makes me a diamond girl?

'Well, thank you Mr Shah...but how's that?'

'Because Cousin Naveen will truly be honoured to take a woman out that will not let him down even if she is not feeling full of health. You have come to me for help and I have let you down. Cousin Naveen owns the pharmacy back home and he may know of another remedy for you. I will tell him straight away and he will be sure to bring something to the date for you! In fact, I will call my other cousin who is looking after the Pharmacy while Naveen is here. Maybe he will know of something too.' Mr Shah reaches into his pocket for his smart phone and starts chattering away in his native tongue, while giving me a thumbs up.

'Oh great. Tell me later.' I give him an abstract wave as I slowly back out of the store. I don't even buy the peach and punch drops. Damn. How could a plan so right go so wrong so quickly? I must really be losing my touch.

Still, all is not lost. As I'm already up I really can just make an early start on the stocktaking. Plus,

I've got all day before I meet Cousin Naveen – plenty of time to devise a plan to make sure our first date... is also our last.

Eight

'Gina? Gina!' Patsy's piercing voice breaks into my thoughts

'Sorry Pat, I was miles away'

'I know you've been here for hours already, but try and keep up boss. I was asking if you wanted the black negligee from the Dark Spice range on the window dummy or the purple Lustylicious three piece with the suspenders?'

She's looking at me patiently but I know she probably just wants to throw the dummy at me.

'The Lustylicious please.'

Patsy is still just staring

'The purple set.' I add.

'I heard you.'

You wouldn't think so by the way she's still standing like a statue. I lift my chin at her

'So?'

'So, what's going on? You've been super distracted all morning.'

She's right. I have been. I still haven't found a way to get out of my date later on. Not to mention I'm still reeling from my failure earlier at Mr Shah's shop.

'Oh, I've just got some stuff on my mind.' Like my first date with Mr Shah's cousin twice removed on his Mother's side from Mumbai. I can't believe it was only last night that my supposed nearest and dearest gathered together to arrange dates for me, and the plan is already in action less than 24 hours later. How's that for project management?

Lisa texted me ten minutes ago and so far they've managed to get me twenty dates. Yes, that's right - *twenty* dates! I mean, are all the internet dating sites down or something? How could they find twenty guys available for dates in less than 24 hours?

'Stuff like your first date later today?' Patsy interrupts my train of thought again and is grinning from ear to ear as she repositions a bra strap.

'It's great that your family and friends are helping you like this. I don't even know why someone who looks as hot as you would even need help. It's crazy to think that you of all people has trouble getting a date!' Patsy is shaking her head as she walks into the stockroom.

'Well, technically I don't need help getting a date – they just don't like that I'm single. But if I'm okay with being on my own, then I really don't see...'

I'm interrupted by a scream from the stockroom.

'Yikes! There is a big old spider back here!' Patsy leaps out of the stockroom and shudders as she reaches under the counter for a red can of Raid and the biggest spray bottle of what smells like...peppermint?

'Take that! And that!' Patsy is firing back into the room at the spider using both sprays like hand guns in an American street gang movie, 'I read that spiders don't like peppermint or conkers.' She stops spraying for a second, 'do we have any conkers?'

'No.' I say with my back turned to her so she can't see the big satisfied smile on my face. That'll teach her for helping out with this date project. Patsy - still armed with her sprays - bends down and stealthily tiptoes back into the stockroom as if anything louder will alert the spider to her whereabouts – if it's still even breathing after that chemical cloud she just infused the room with.

'Anyway, back to your date thing. So when your friend Lisa asked me to help I couldn't really say no to helping my boss, could I?'

'Well, technically you could have.' I mumble under my breath.

'Sorry, I didn't catch that?'

'Erm...I just coughed. Ahack, ahack. You were saying?'

'Yes, I was saying I told her I'd jump at the chance to help my boss find a fella. Hey! I've just had a brainwave! What if you did a modelling event for the new lingerie lines like you used to when you first opened up the shop? You still look hot and it's bound to draw a crowd of men as well as women. We already know that plenty of guys buy lingerie as pressies.'

'Yes. For their girlfriends!'

'Not all for their girlfriends. Some just buy them for their one night friends as a thank you.' I can't see her, but I know she's looking like a smug little know-it-all back there.

'And that's your idea of potential partner material is it?' I roll my eyes and shake my head.

Patsy pops her head out of the stockroom, 'They wouldn't be like that with you. Look at you. You're enough for married men to want to leave their wives. You'd have no problem getting a single guy to gladly relinquish *that* status.' Her eyes are gleaming as she disappears again. If only. Sigh. Patsy is ever the hopeless romantic. If I was trying to hook someone up I would definitely have her on my team. Damn that Lisa again.

'Seriously. You should think about doing another show.'

'Hmm, I don't know if I want to go back to relive those days again.'

'Why on earth not? I mean, I know the catalogue you commission is good marketing, but have you forgotten the queue of girls AND guys that bought the Booty Cutie line after they saw you modelling it *live* at one of your pageants?'

'And have you forgotten some of the stand-out characters we had to deal with that came from that same queue? Like the spray tanned guy...'

'Yes sir, good choice. Your partner will love the Moulin Noir set. So, what bust size are you looking for?'

'Erm, something small. Very small. More or less flat chested actually.'

'Hmm...maybe an A cup?' Patsy suggests

'Howabout a No cup?' Spray tanned guy howls with laughter.

Patsy joins in, 'That small huh? I'll have a look outback and see what we've got. Now, what size knickers? If they're that small on top, I'm thinking an extra small for below too?'

'On the contrary, I'm thinking a large. Extra-large if you have it.'

'Really?!' Patsy opens her eyes wide in surprise, 'Erm...possibly that range might go up to that...size. I'll check that out too. Would you like it gift-wrapped?'

'Oh, that would be a nice touch!' Spray tanned guy gives a big smile.

'And the card? I should make it out to Ms...?'

'You should make it out to **Mr**, darling!'

I can hear Patsy giggling in the back, 'Now, who could forget that! But that was a one-off!'

'Well let me give you a two-off – like that short guy that came a bit later in the navy suit...'

'So sir, you've decided on the SexCess set. It's a customer favourite that's for sure. Really sexy, just like the name.' I start to wrap the delicate lacy set in tissue paper.

'When I saw you modelling it on that calendar you made, I instantly knew it was the one for her!' Navy suit guy nods knowingly.

'And the cups have a subtle padding in them especially for the smaller ladies. She'll have uber boobies when she puts this on.'

'That's exactly what I was thinking!' Navy suit guy nods even more, almost resembling a Mr Bobble Head.

'The matching thongs are extra comfy. She'll hardly notice she's wearing them'

'Oh, she will be really pleased about that. Some of her other ones she says really "ride up".'

'This is a lovely gift. She's a lucky lady.'

'Nothing but the best for my Nanna!'

'Oh yeah! Now that was one creepy guy...' Patsy comes back out again hands on hip, still grasping her spider-killing tools, 'Okay, you win.' Patsy finally concedes that her idea is not going to come back into fruition any time soon, shrugs her shoulders and disappears back into the stock-room.

'Oh yeah, before I forget, your friend Lisa asked me to check your work schedule a couple weeks ago. I hope you didn't mind?' Patsy pops her head around the door again.

'Why on earth would I mind?' I manage to ground out through gritted teeth and a strained smile. How mad can I really be? In her mind, she's helping. In my mind, I could cheerfully throttle her.

'That on top of your generous offer to keep a look out for single guys too. How *sweet* of you.' I can barely hold back my sarcasm.

'I didn't want to say yet...but I've actually found you someone already!'

I quickly walk into the store room to see Patsy bobbing up and down as if she'll burst if she doesn't tell me. Before I can open my mouth to hazard a guess she squeals, 'Dave!'

'Dave...?'

'Yes! Dave!'

'Which Dave? Dave who works at Accounts 4 U?'

'No, the other one.'

I crinkle my nose in thought. I don't even know why I care.

'Dave with the false American accent?'

'Ooh, I forgot about him. I should give his name to Lisa actually, as he's single. He came in yesterday after you'd left but he sounded Australian that time. But, no not him. The *other* Dave.'

I am really straining to think who she is talking about. There is only one other Dave that comes to mind but that would be absurd.

'You can't mean Dave who orders lingerie every other week that's never the same size?'

'Yes, that's the one! I swear he gets cuter every time I see him' Patsy is now all dreamy-eyed. She rushes on to stop the barrage of objections she knows are ready to spill out of me.

'We know he likes dating, he's clearly very generous with his gifts and my great grandmother told me once that if a guy isn't married, he's single. If anyone could take him off the market Gina, it's you!'

'Who says I want to take him or anyone else off the market?' I splutter before I can stop myself.

'Lisa said when we all first talked about doing this for you two weeks ago, that all single guys are to be put forward. She said you'd be fine with it.'

Patsy leans slowly towards the shelf again to check for signs of life from the spider.

I turn and walk back to the store front without saying another word because if I do, I'll surely choke on it. A customer walks in which gives me a chance to focus on something other than my no good do-gooder assistant.

'Well hello. It's a rare treat to see the boss serving behind the counter.' The customer saunters up to the counter in a red baseball cap and huge dark sunglasses.

'I'm sorry, have we met?' I'm straining to try and recognise who is behind the huge sunglasses with no luck.

'Hey, Dave is that you? I recognised your voice.' Patsy pops her head out of the stock room, 'we were just talking about you!'

'Oh, you were, were you?' He's answering her, but his huge sunglasses are fixed in my direction. It's all I can do to only flush a mild pink rather than full blown red.

'What's with the disguise?' Patsy asks before disappearing back into the stockroom.

'I'm incognito today. Trying to avoid Milly from...' Dave realises I am staring un-amused and coughs to end his conversation.

'Can I help you with something?' I'm certainly not going to call him sir and Dave sounds a little more familiar than I want to be. I'll think I'll stick with calling him... nothing.

'Yes! Yes, you can. I just wanted to change the size of my...er my order. Same set, just 34D instead of 34B.' He talks about ladies underwear like he's talking about the weather.

'Patsy knows all the details. I'm a regular.'

'So, I've heard.' I add a fixed smile to my face.

'Don't worry Dave, I'll make the changes. I've got you covered.' Patsy's voice wafts from the stockroom

'Thanks Pat, you're a star. If only there were more out there like you.' He gives me a suggestive smile, mine stays fixed.

'Oh stop, Dave!' Patsy's coy giggle emits from the stockroom. It takes a humungous effort on my part to not roll my eyes. Dave knocks twice on the counter in acknowledgement, gives me a little bow and saunters out in the same way that he sauntered in.

So this is the guy that Patsy wants to volunteer to set me up on a date with – in the flesh. Not if I have anything to do with it. Suddenly, the realisation hits me. If this type of guy can make the dating list, then they really are as determined to get me hitched as I am determined to stay single. That means if I'm really going to keep my secret, a secret – then this means war.

Nine

Only a few more hours before Project Datelock officially begins and I now know exactly how I'll deal with Cousin Naveen. I don't know why I didn't think of it immediately, it's so obvious! Clearly, he'll be looking for wife material – so I'll make sure I'm the most un-wifely person he's ever met.

Plus, just for going on a date with him, Mr Shah will probably feel obliged to throw in a few free bags of Skittles or some of those new peach and punch drops I didn't get to buy this morning. They looked really nice.

My phone rings and startles me. I really must change that Jaws ring tone Gran put on my phone the minute she learned how to download ring tones. The Sound of Music she put on Mum's, or Match of the Day on Dad's would be preferable to this one. I see Mr Shah's number flashing at me on the caller ID. I suddenly wish he were calling to cancel but not even I could be so lucky.

'Hi, Mr Shah.'

'Oh hello, Gina dear. I am having very bad news I'm afraid. Cousin Naveen will not be making it to meet you.'

I hold my breath. There IS a man upstairs! I believe! Relief floods over me – free skittles just can't compete with this feeling! And I wasn't the one that cancelled so Lisa can't accuse me of anything!

'Oh, I'm *so* sorry to hear that.'

I heard that when you smile people can sense it on the phone. I hope that's just a vicious rumour.

'Yes, my dear. My sister has found him a nice wife back in India. He is taking flight straight back home to marry her next week.'

'Oh, congratulations to him. I couldn't be happier to hear the news!' And believe me when I say, I really *really* mean that.

'But never be fearing – I am also having very good news!'

'Good news?'

'Yes, I have spoken to Roger just this afternoon and he is agreeing to take you out now in place of Cousin Naveen.'

'Erm...Roger?'

'Oh yes, he cashes his unemployment cheque in post office every other Friday at two o'clock. After hearing news from Cousin Naveen, Roger came into post office. I tell him about you and he agree to take you out. He is very much gentleman. What wonderful news is this, yes?'

I don't think sensing people smiling down the phone is a rumour after all because I can literally *feel* Mr Shah beaming at the other end of the line.

'Mr Shah – I couldn't possibly expect this Roger fellow to spend half of his unemployment income on me. That wouldn't be right.'

According to Lisa's stipulations about my dating regime, I have to accept every date that is offered to me. She didn't say anything about trying to persuade a date replacement to not fritter away a chunk of his fortnightly dosh on one meal.

'But he is so very much looking forward to taking you for nice food. I am telling him what lovely girl you are and also *Lisa* is telling me that you are liking meeting new people and Roger is very much liking meeting new people also.'

Oh, oh. I'm not sure I liked the way he emphasised Lisa's name just now. Did he just name-drop her to let me know that he knows she mustn't know I had a date offer that I didn't take? Darn it. I can't take the chance.

'I guess if this Roger fellow is prepared to sacrifice some of his limited funds to take me out, how can I not sacrifice an evening in return?' I give a little laugh that sounds pitiful even to my own ears.

'Oh, this is good news. You will be having very good time. So, you will be meeting him at Nando's on the High Road little bit earlier at four o clock instead of five. Lisa is telling me this is no problem for you because your assistant Patsy will stay late for you.' Well, if it isn't Lisa to the rescue again. And as for that Patsy, I see another eight-legged creature in her future.

'Roger is also telling me for you to be meeting him there will be easiest. Now you can drink plenty water so that your stomach will be feeling better. I call my other cousin and he says this is good.'

'My stomach?'

'Yes. Your stomach was still upset earlier from last night?'

Geez, I'd completely forgotten my failed excuse!

'Yes! yes, Mr Shah – I'll drink lots of water right now. I can hardly wait. I'll be there.'

I actually sing the word "the-ere" to give some oomph to the enthusiasm I'm not quite feeling. I know I wanted to get out of the date with Cousin Naveen, but not so that I'd end up on another date in his place.

Despite everything, there's still one good thing about later.

Nando's. I mean who doesn't like chicken, right?

Ten

So, here I am. Waiting for Roger outside Nando's. I had to make sure my appearance was as undesirable as I could make it with the contents of my wardrobe. My jeans have rips across the knees – I had to put the rips there myself and fray them a bit for authenticity. I think it looks like genuine wear and tear now.

I didn't wash my hair last night to make sure it had a bit of a lank look today and put lots of product in. But I think I overdid it with the product because it feels so greasy that I can't stand it touching my neck. I've had to put it up in a high ponytail. My plain shirt I'm sure screams SALE and not because it's one of my greatest bargains to date – 70% off! – but because it is *really* plain. Now I think about it, I'm not even sure why I bought it...oh yes, because it was a great bargain and what other reason do you really need?

Okay, he's a little late. I look at my watch again. Okay, he's more than a little late - 45 minutes to be exact, but I can't bail because it's not his fault. Roger texted Mr Shah who texted Lisa who texted me to say there's a broken down lorry and his bus has been diverted. Oh, actually, I think that might be him getting off the 247 bus now. Mr Shah said he had long, brown hair. This guy has long hair which looks more ginger than brown but that could be down to the light. As he gets closer, he stares down his nose at me.

'Hi, I'm Roger. Are you Gina?'

Yep, he's definitely ginger, but a kind of mousy ginger. Quite an unusual shade actually.

'Yes, that's me – pleased to meet you'

I give a little smile and hold out my hand to shake which he grasps and shakes so hard that the rest of me goes up and down too.

'Hey, can we go to the MacDonalds instead? It's just that I have to make my cheque last and I have a two-for-one voucher that runs out today.'

'Oh...Sure.' From Nando's to MacDonalds? Hmm.

Luckily, the MacDonalds is only two shops down, so we make the 8 step journey in silence.

'Shall we?' He points to the MacDonalds door and then walks straight through, letting it swing back practically hitting me in the face! As I pull the door open again, he turns around and starts walking backwards towards the counter.

'I won't insult you by treating you like an inferior female who needs a big strong man,' he holds up his fingers to do imaginary quote marks, 'to hold open a door for them. I'm all about equality.'

And there was I thinking it was just good manners. I give a cautious smile. I notice that he's also wearing jeans that are frayed at the knee...and the foot...and at the side...but then again, he is unemployed so maybe his income can't stretch to new jeans. Yet it can to taking some strange woman he's never met to eat out...oh, but he's got a two-for-one voucher. It's actually quite touching that he's prepared to share it with someone he barely knows.

His hair is longer than I would have thought – in fact, quite a bit longer than mine and tied back in a neat but rather high ponytail too. A rather unusual hairstyle for a guy I think, but each to their own.

I'm starting to feel a little more positive about sabotaging this evening. We already have tatty jeans, equality for women, and high ponytails in common so maybe I can keep him focused on that. Then maybe later I can steer the conversation towards politics with a twist of religion (who says these topics are no no's?). That should keep us from straying into...ahem...*other* realms of conversation.

'I'd like a Big Mac, a Filet-o-fish, a cheeseburger, large fries, and small fries,' he turns to me, 'large fries are just not quite enough, you know?' then he turns back to the cashier, 'and an extra-large diet Pepsi. And for you?' Roger swings around from the cashier again.

As I rummage in my bag for my glasses to look at the sky high menu, Roger taps my shoulder and double raises his eyebrows.

'Or we could share?'

A sort of twisted grin is on his face and I'm not sure if he's trying to seduce me or scare me into accepting his offer. I know his funds are limited but he's got a two-for-one voucher for goodness sake.

'Well, I wouldn't want to deprive you of some of your large fries and small fries especially if that's just enough for you. So, can I just have a cheeseburger please? My own, if that's okay?'

Roger shrugs his shoulders and turns back to the cashier.

'That'll be £12.45 please.'

Roger hands over the voucher.

'I'm sorry sir; this voucher ran out two days ago.' The cashier looks at Roger who does a good job of feigning surprise and starts to squint at the date on the voucher.

'Damn.' Is all he manages to say to that. He then rummages around in his pockets and pulls out a £5 note and puts a handful of assorted coins on the counter which he starts to pick through.

'I was just thinking that maybe we could go dutch? You know, first meeting and all. That's fair, right?'

'Oh! ...okay. Sure.' I get a tenner out of my purse and thrust it towards the cashier at the same time Roger hands him his fiver. I'm not put out in the slightest. It *is* fair.

'We're a little short staffed today. Jennifer and Devon both called in sick. Some would say that's a coincidence. I say whatever,' the cashier rolls his eyes, 'anyway, find a seat and I'll bring your order over.' The cashier gives me a big smile as he taps into the till and takes out some change which

Roger boldly accepts and puts into his pocket. He turns to me as if all is well with the world

'There's a spare table over there, shall we?'

I smile and lead the way towards said table, saying a mantra in my mind of '...let the change go...just let the change go...'

As we sit, Roger leans back and just stares at me. I guess it's over to me to break the silence.

'So, Roger. You're in between jobs at the moment?'

'Yeah, I need something that can be incorporated into my routine. The nine to five grind is not for me. That's the Government's way of reducing the population.' He suddenly leans forward, 'I mean it's not even nine to five anymore is it? Longer hours, no weekends off, less pay – they are trying to work us to death to make their plan come true and most of us are not even trying to fight it!' He bangs his fist on the table which makes me jump.

'Umm, how about something part-time? Like in a bar? That doesn't sound too life-draining? Might even be fun, meeting lots of new people, lots of *girls*...' I end, subtly

'Oh please!' Roger flicks the air *and* his ponytail, a look of pure disdain on his face and slouches back into his chair again

'The government knows that alcohol is one of the roads to ruin. Why would I help them with their plan by deliberately administering one of the temptations they use to control society?'

I think carefully before responding and frankly, I'm at a loss for words. Then as if by magic, I'm saved by my burger, placed almost reverently in front of me with the same big smile by the same cashier who sort of dumps Roger's in front of him, causing a few chips to jump out of the bag onto the tray. Roger puts the small fries and the large fries together in one big pile. He tears open several packets of tomato ketchup – I would say he has approximately ten in front of him – and then proceeds to drown the fries. I go to take a bite of my burger, but before it touches my lips, he forcefully continues.

'...you see, the government wants to create a nanny state, where they are in control of every aspect of our lives and...'

While he's in nanny state mode, I try again to get started on my burger when he suddenly bangs the table again with his free hand.

'...I mean can you believe that they want us to believe they have our best interests at heart? Yeah, right. Look at...'

After three more attempts to start my burger, and Roger up to his last few fries, comes the moment of dread.

'So, what's your story anyway? How comes a lady like you needs hooking up by their local postmaster?'

I finally managed to take a bite and now I'm spluttering it back up like I'm five years old. The cashier jumps out from no-where to violently pat me on the back and wipe his hand across my forehead.

'Are you okay? Do you need mouth to mouth?' he says staring at my mouth with intent.

'No! Thank you. I'm okay.' The cashier walks away with a concerned smile for me and a frown for Roger, who shrugs his shoulders

'I could see he had it in hand,' a slight red tinge creeps into his cheeks.

I hold my chest and take a few deep breaths to buy a bit more time to answer his question.

'So, what were you saying? Oh yes, I guess I've just not met Mr Right yet.'

Roger is looking slitty eyed at me now 'Hmm...really? I would have thought someone like you would have met five or more Mr Rights a day.'

'Yeah, but Mr Right soon turns into Mr Wrong when you tell him that your calling is to one day be a female monk. You know, like a nun.'

Roger's slitty eyes are now open wide, so I know I'm now in no-second-date territory.

'...that serene life of peace and tranquillity just makes me feel at one with nature. And it takes a certain type of man to want to join you on that path of lifelong celibacy...' I lean forward to stare softly at Roger, who appears speechless for the first time since I've met him.

Suddenly, the alarm on his phone starts beeping and he looks almost relieved 'Sorry, gotta go, that's my signing on alarm'

'Signing on alarm?'

'Yeah, for my unemployment cheque.' Roger does some finger quotes in the air as he says un-employment cheque. 'The government makes us sign to prove we're worthy. My forefathers paid into this system – and now they are gone and can't collect what's due to them, it's my duty to make sure I do. The politicians aren't going to get the chance to squander their legacy on my watch.' Roger bangs his fist on the table again. You'd think I'd be used to it by now, but it still makes me jump and nearly bite my tongue instead of the burger.

'Anyway, they changed my appointment to a late night one today, that's why I told Mr Shah I could take you out. Hey, you wouldn't happen to have some loose change would you? My Oyster card is a little short.'

As is his memory. I know he can't have forgotten that he's already got my loose change! I take a deep breath and start my mantra again 'let the change go...let the change go...' while I take a couple of pound coins out of my purse. He pushes away his chair and leans over me as he reaches for my coins.

'Shame, I'm already on a path to make sure Big Brother doesn't pull the wool over my eyes. But good luck on your nun-hood. Look! There's my bus!' And with that, he and his high ponytail fly out the door together. The cashier arrives back with some water as I take a huge burger bite and smirk to myself. That's one down.

* * *

'Lisa, it was the biggest disaster, I kid you not!'

I can tell she is near to tears of laughter at the other end of the phone.

'I can't believe he took your change!' she collapses into a fit of giggles. Try as I might to stay stern, it's not long before I'm joining her.

'Yes, and he told me that we were all being turned into clones through satellite TV!'

We are both hooting down the phone now. After a good minute, we both seem to catch our breaths.

'And after all that, he just left? No talk about meeting again?' Lisa sounds surprised now.

'Yep. Said he had to sign on, and off he went.'

'And Mr Shah said this Roger guy was so looking forward to the date too.'

'Yeah, it was nice of him to step in at such short notice. But, in all honesty, I don't think I was really his type'

'You're practically everyone's type, Gina.' Lisa sounds a little baffled.

'Not this guy's. When I started talking about the future, he was having "nun" of it.'

Eleven

A week has passed since this charade began, and it's time to meet everyone again. By the time I arrive home for the second date meeting, everyone else has already arrived and clearly made themselves at home in my home. Gran has made herself a sandwich and Delilah is nibbling on a square of my Tesco's Finest Chocolate. I guess that's the end of my plan to eat that later with a cup of tea.

Lisa rubs her hands together and consults her clip board.

'Okay everyone, I know we've had lots of suggestions – thank you all for that – and a great list of potentials all eager to date our girl,' Lisa gives me a big wink, 'but I think we'll start the ball rolling today with your preferred candidate Mrs Robbins – who is...' Lisa scans down the page '...Stuart!'

Mum punches the air like she's won a competition.

'Glad you're so chuffed to set up your only child up with a total stranger who could possibly be a psychopath with killer tendencies, Mum.'

'He's not a stranger! And he's certainly not a psychopath!' I do believe my mother actually sounds *offended* that I could suggest such a thing. This on its own would usually worry me, if I wasn't more concerned that she didn't also defend the possibility that he might have killer tendencies.

'He's a young man I've known for a while and I always thought he'd make a lovely son-in-law.' Mum's eyes take on a dreamy glaze.

'She does know it's just a date, right?' I loudly whisper to Lisa who simply smiles and waves her hand towards me to not worry.

'Me and your father met on *just a date* forty years ago and look at us now.' Mum crosses her arms proudly.

I look over at Dad who is engrossed in my latest edition of Look magazine and mumbling to himself about the price of a bag he's just seen in it. Mum, on the other hand, is a little too excited for my liking at the chance to be involved in choosing a potential son-in-law.

'Aww, how romantic Mrs Robbins' Lisa gives mum a wide smile 'I look at you and Mr Robbins and I can see why you'd want that for your daughter. Tell us some more about this Stuart.'

'Well, everyone calls him Stu and he drives the 247 bus. I see him most mornings when I catch his bus to go to that new mini supermarket to get the milk.'

Mr Shah's face falls, 'You are not liking my milk, Mrs Robbins?'

'Of course your milk is absolutely fine, Mr Shah, but you don't stock that new lactose intolerant, dairy free, fat free, non-cream, calcium fortified brand that Mr Robbins needs to drink because of his "condition".' Mum bends the first two fingers on both hands in the air to emphasise "condition". Mr Shah nods in understanding. I look towards my Dad in confusion. I didn't even know he had a "condition". Dad looks up too as if it's the first time he's also hearing about this "condition", shrugs his shoulder at me, then continues reading.

'Stu is always on time. He always helps me with my bags. He always has a lovely smile, and always says "Good Morning Mrs Robbins" whenever he sees me. He always drops me off just before the bus stop so I don't have to walk too far back to the house and...'

I interrupt 'Okay, okay Mum, he sounds great.'
What I really want to say is that he sounds like a
brand of sanitary towel but I manage to hold that
in.

Mum keeps going as if I never spoke '...he always
asks about your father. He'll have been single for
eight months on Monday – the last date he went
on was a disaster, the young lady kept spraying
him with breadstick crumbs every time she spoke!'

Wow...so speaking and spraying breadcrumbs
is actually a phenomenon not just limited to the
Harolds of this world - who knew!

'He's been ready to settle down for a while but
just hasn't met the right girl.' Mum gives a sad look
as if it's a crying shame he hasn't been snapped up
yet.

'Until he meets our Gina' Lisa pipes up 'He
sounds perfect for any girl, Mrs Robbins.'

Mum instantly perks up again at the comment.

'That may be so,' I interrupt again, this time
with more force 'but what do you see that is so
specifically perfect for me?'

'Isn't it obvious dear?' Mum looks genuinely
perplexed that a light bulb hasn't lit up over my
head.

'If a guy has that much respect for your mother, then of course he'll have just as much respect for her daughter. Isn't that right, Henry?' Mum looks over at Dad, 'Henry!' Mum shouts. Dad looks up from the magazine and taps the top of the page.

'Your mother is right, love. It says as much right here in this article

- How to turn a Mummy's boy into a Man's man. I'll let you have a read when I'm done.'

I scan the room to see everyone staring at my mother as if she has just spouted some profound words of wisdom...which, I suppose she has when you really think about it.

'Just to let you know, I've already given Gina's business card to Stu and showed him her picture...did you get that bit down love?' Mum and Lisa now have their heads together with Lisa scribbling notes.

'...he's going to call you on Sunday evening to finalise plans. Lisa suggested that Rymans bar place might be nice at around 8pm as that's happy hour too - so I fed that back like you told me dear.' Lisa gives my Mum a congratulatory thumbs up, to which Mum puffs out her chest in pride, clearly feeling her actions have been very important.

'I thought Sunday would be a good day for a respectable date with a lovely young man.' Mum crosses her arms in emphasis.

'Not to mention it will give Gina a few days to touch up her roots, I think I see a few greys coming through...' Delilah adds before popping another square of *my* chocolate in her mouth.

'You do not see any such thing!' I leave off adding "you cow" as I jump off the sofa and run to the mirror. 'And anyway, how do you lot know if I'm even free on...'

Gran waves my personal diary at me, stopping me mid-sentence. I'd forgotten they already know I'm free most evenings.

'Well, that's fine then. Just wanted to be sure.' I say in what I hope is a convincing unbothered manner.

I look in the mirror again, and sure enough, I can see a few greys glistening near my scalp. It would have to be that Have-a-dig Delilah that noticed them. But now I think about it, they actually might work in my favour. I mean, I don't want to give the impression that I've spruced up to the nines for this date, do I? Especially with my secret at stake. A plan starts to form in my head about how to deal with this date. I smile to myself. Super Stu won't know what hit him.

Twelve

'...No Mum, I'm not going to wear a hat. If a few grey hairs bother Stu, then maybe he's not prospective son-in-law material after all.'

'...Yes Mum; I will wear some of the Lavender Spritzer you bought me for Christmas too. I'm sure if Dad loves it then Stu will too.'

'...Of course I'm wearing clean underwear, Mum. Believe it or not, I do that even if I'm not on a date.'

Geez, Mum is driving me nuts. Every day since she arranged for me to go on this date with Stu, she's been calling about everything, from whether I've shaved my legs to if I'm using extra minty fresh toothpaste. Sunday has not come quick enough.

I'm beginning to think that she's pinned all her hopes of having grandkids on this guy.

This Stuart guy sounds almost too good to be true so I don't know why she's so worried. Not only does he drive the 247 bus she takes to the supermarket that sells the lactose intolerant, dairy free, fat free, non-cream, calcium fortified milk she buys for Dad, but just the other day he held the bus for ten minutes while she looked for her Freedom Pass. I mean, I'm half expecting this guy to wear a halo.

My phone rings again for like the hundredth time.

'Mum, I already told you...' but the voice on the other end is not Mum's.

'Hi, Gina? It's Stuart. Stuart Harrison?' Oh shit.

'Stuart! Hi. Yes. I'm so sorry; I thought you were my Mum again telling me to...' I stop mid-sentence. He doesn't really need to know my mother just called to tell me to make sure I don't pass wind in front of him, now does he?

'To?' he prompts

'To...remind me not to forget my keys. I locked myself out the other day.' When I was 11, but this is a minor detail that he doesn't need to know.

'So, what's up? Calling to cancel?' I joke, but really mean it.

'Ha ha, actually no. I was just calling to tell you I'll be wearing a white carnation. Thought it would make it a little easier to spot me in the crowd.'

Little does he know, I can already spot him in a crowd from a mile away. Mum's descriptive powers would make her a prize asset to the police if she ever witnessed a criminal in the act...

'He's not quite 6ft, more like 5ft 10 and he's got these chocolate brown eyes – very McVities. I think the left one is slightly larger than the right one, but he's assured me it doesn't stop him from seeing me at the bus stop...' (She actually goes a bit gooey when she says that).

'His hair is a nice shiny Demerara sugar brown which could do with a bit of a cut, but he says he's doing the late shift on the buses at the moment so it's hard to catch the barber by the time he's finished. I did tell him I used to do hair back in the day so would be happy to give him a trim.'

Who needs a flower after that?

'That's a great idea, not sure how I'd have recognised you. Are we still okay for 8.00pm at Rymans Bar?'

'Absolutely.'

'Okay, see you there.'

Damn it, he even sounds like a good guy. And that's bad. Good guys make you feel all warm and fuzzy, and when you feel warm and fuzzy you start opening up – and when you start opening up, you start saying things you didn't plan to say. The date hasn't even started yet and already I feel the pressure of making sure I stick to the things I plan to say, no matter what. I can't wait for this whole find-me-a date thing to be over.

I really need to talk to Lisa again to try and persuade her that I can find the right guy on my own without help from her and everyone else even though their offer of help is appreciated. Of course, their help isn't *really* appreciated, but telling her that won't have the same ring to it.

Okay, only two hours left to go from Glam Gina to Plain Jane and I'm having a bad hair day. You might think a bad hair day means when your hair is looking its worst. But a bad hair day today for me, is when the bloomin' thing won't behave the way I want it to! Three days I've gone without washing it so it should look all lank and limp, but instead it looks as if I've just stepped out of the hairdresser! Stupid Super Shampoo. I mean who wants hair that still looks shiny after three days anyway? Okay, *usually* I would but not today of all days, especially when shiny is exactly the opposite of the look I was going for. Trust me to choose the one product that lives up to its claims.

I peer hard into the mirror, wishing that a zit or two would magically appear. I've even tried to find something suitably unsuitable in my wardrobe but this shirt I bought from that Second Time Around store on the high street looks design-er...actually, now I'm really studying it, I just may have struck lucky with this. The stitching is really...what am I thinking? Focus Gina because you are being cursed with nothing going your way so far today. Along with phones that won't stop bloody ringing! I grab it in a huff.

'Yes? Yes, Mum, I won't have spinach in case it gets caught in my teeth like the time I did my winning speech at the 13th Annual Beauty Pageant for English Belles. And yes, I will tell Stu that you said Hi.'

Geez, Mum is more nervous about this date than me and she doesn't even have a secret...well, only that she has a crush on Steve McGarrett from New Hawaii Five O. She totally denies it when Dad's around, but the glazed look in her eyes when the new Steve steps on screen always gives her away.

My phone is ringing again. I make an instant decision that if it's Mum again, it's going straight to voicemail. Caller ID shows that it's Lisa. I'm considering still letting it go to voicemail. More "helpful" advice is exactly what I don't need right now...then again if I don't answer, Lisa will think something is up and might decide to come round in person. An idea I like even less.

'Lisa.'

'Gina?'

'Uh huh.'

'Nervous?'

'Why?'

'Checking.'

'Oh.'

'So?'

'No.'

'Sure?'

'Sure.'

'Okay.'

'Okay.'

'Bye.'

'Bye.'

That's got to be a contender for the shortest conversation ever between me and Lisa.

Right. This phone is being switched off until I am at Rymans bar. All these calls are putting me off my game. And it's a game I have to lose.

Thirteen

Okay, I am here at Rymans Bar. It looks nice. Ambient. Will probably look just as nice from the inside which is where I need to go. Like right now. Deep breath. Just look for the white carnation. Be cool and he will end up a friend just like all the others. Even if Lisa and my whole family are suddenly in control of who I date, they can't control the outcomes.

I push open the door. Straight away I see a white carnation. But it has to be a mistake. No way would my mother choose this guy to be the potential father of her grandchildren...would she? That is not a 6ft someone. I mean I hope he's sitting down but I actually think he might be standing up? As I look down, I can confirm those are definitely Cuban heels touching the ground. Quite a stylish pair too I might add. I wonder if they do a female version...unless those are the female version?

I don't have far to look back up to see a rather large lady envelope him in a hug. I can see a carnation delicately balancing in her cleavage, just above his head which is now squashed between her two...well, you can imagine I'm sure.

I have a quick browse and see three other people with carnations – one is wearing four of the flowers. Clearly they don't want to be missed. I make a beeline for the nearest vacant stool and take a relieved breath that my mother's observational skills aren't out of whack because none of these people look like who she described.

Looking at my watch, I can see he's ten minutes late. I'm sure I read somewhere that fifteen minutes is acceptable to be late and any time after sixteen minutes is acceptable to leave. I feel a flutter of excitement. Is getting out of this date really going to be so simple? My palms are sweating in anticipation. I could be out of this situation in...I quickly look at my watch again...two minutes and forty-two seconds. I start tapping my fingers on the bar in agitation then my feet follow, tapping against the footstool to the same beat. Then I start humming "I've got two more minutes to go" to the rhythm of So Solid's 29 seconds.

The bartender gives me a strange look. In fact, it's a similar look to the man on my left. The woman on my right is nodding in time to my humming as if she wants to hum along with me.

I grab the glass next to me and gulp down a mouthful. The man on my left is now smiling at me and picks up the same glass I've just put back down and slowly puts it to his lips. Then winks at me. It then dawns on me that I didn't actually order a drink. He's now looking at me as if I've given him some sort of mating signal. If the ground were to swallow me up right now, it would spit me back out again because my embarrassment would be too much for it to take.

I drop my purse on the floor and awkwardly climb down from my bar stool to pick it up. I accidentally-on-purpose kick it in front of me and when I reach down to pick it up, I arise three stools down. I slip and slide onto the stool now closest to me and look at my watch again – 1 minute and twenty seconds to go. I look at the floor, then my shoes – some rather comfy patent courts I might add – then back at my watch. And just like the song, I have got just 29 seconds to go! Sod it, I'm off.

Before I can even swivel my chair towards the exit, I feel a tap on my shoulder and freeze, hoping that it's not the guy three stools down offering me another sip of his drink. I cautiously look over my shoulder to be met with the brightest Colgate smile – all even and blindingly white... and a carnation. My eyes wander downwards – and yep, no Cubans.

'Erm...I'm up here?'

Startled, my eyes jump up to his to be met with that super bright smile again.

'Gina, right? You haven't changed much.' He takes out a picture of me and puts it beside my face to compare. I divert just my eyes to look at it, to see it's me on my graduation when I was nineteen! Really, Mum? – I know it's your favourite picture of me, but come on. I stare at him again, kind of dumbstruck. He looks exactly how Mum described him.

'Yes, yes – I'm Gina. Your voice hasn't changed much from the phone call either so you must be Stuart.' He beams at me again and it takes all my effort not to squint.

'Sorry I'm late. I helped one of my elderly route regulars take her shopping into her house when one of the wheels came off her shopping trolley.' He smiles apologetically, and this time, I do squint, but as discreetly as one can when it comes to squinting.

'Can I get you a drink?' As he signals to the bartender, I give him a quick once over. Levi Jeans, rather sensible shoes – he probably wears them to work too - with a simple blue t-shirt and black bomber jacket. His eyes are a deep dark brown just like Mum said, but I'd say more Bourneville than McVities.

'Drink?' Stuart raises his eyebrow at me. The one that's over the bigger eye. Mum was spot on with that too.

'Sure. A wine spritzer please.'

To be honest, I'm not even sure what a spritzer actually is – but I've always thought it sounded really sophisticated. As the bar tender brings back the drinks, I notice Mr Glass-sharer give Stuart the once over, shake his head slowly at me and smile into his glass. I straighten up indignantly – who does he think he is to smirk at my date? I deliberately shift in my seat so that he can see me give

Stuart a beaming smile – it's not quite as Colgate as his but decent enough.

'So, Gina. Why does a girl who looks like you need their mother to set them up on a date?'

I can see Mr Glass-sharer choke on his drink from the corner of my eye. Clearly he overheard the question. Nosy so and so. Admittedly, I am a little taken aback myself. Who asks questions like that straight off the bat? What happened to "What do you do?" or "How's your day been?"

'Well, I could answer because a guy like you needed my mum to set him up on a date.' Take that, cheeky sod.

'Touché!' Stuart chuckles. And instantly the ice is broken. After that, we progress with the regular "What do you do?" and "How's your day been?" I'm actually feeling relaxed now and having quite a nice time, but as always, up pops that age old question that can never just lay down and die.

'So Gina, you never did answer my question. So let me rephrase it slightly so as not to cause offence. You're a beautiful girl with a personality to match...' I can't believe I'm blushing at the compliment

'...and I've been trying to work out for the past couple hours why you are single.'

'Well, I guess I haven't met the right guy yet, or maybe I'm just too picky. That's what my Mum always says so it must be true.' I give a little laugh and pretend to sip my drink.

'Your Mother also says that with the number of guys that show an interest in you, she doesn't know why you haven't managed to give her at least four grandkids by now. She thinks you might be looking for something that doesn't exist.' Stuart beams into his glass. I swear the glare from his teeth is bouncing off the glass. He's getting a little too close to that area of conversation that I really don't want to venture in.

'That's Mums for you. I mean, why would anyone look for something that doesn't exist?' I contort my face into a crazy look, shrug my shoulders and hope that he doesn't notice the nervousness that has crept into my voice. It's about time to make my excuses I think.

'Well, what other explanation could there be?' Stuart looks genuinely perplexed. Which is actually quite sweet. I look at him and then into the glass that I'm twisting between my fingers. Could I tell him? He's been quite easy to talk to so far. Surprisingly so. Have I finally found someone I can reveal my secret to? I take a deep breath.

"Well, Stu…if you must know…the reason why I'm single is because I…because…'

To my horror, the words won't come out. They are stuck on the very tip of my tongue and will simply go no further.

'Because you…?' Stuart prompts, concentrating on my lips. I can feel him willing the words within me to fall out. Now my vocal cords are tensing up and I'm feeling hot and bothered. This is crazy. I take a few more deep breaths and another gulp from my glass to steady myself. I try again.

'I'm still single because…because I…I…' Damn it. 'Because I like to travel.' I finally blurt out.

Stuart is still concentrating on my lips, still waiting for more.

'I'd like to travel to third world countries to give aid. I would like to stay in the villages that need it most, so that I could fully appreciate their conditions.'

'Oh…really?'

'Yes. I saw a program with a woman who caught a strain of diphtheria helping out in Nepal. But she'd been vaccinated beforehand so only had diarrhoea for 2 days.'

'Oh…really?'

'Yeah. I guess that's my dream. The helping, not the diarrhoea.'

'Oh...really.'

'Mm, hmm.' I couldn't tell him the true story, so the alternative was to stick with the pre-planned story. I know it's for the best. He probably couldn't handle my secret anyway.

'So, what do you think about travelling Stu?'

'I must admit I wouldn't be too fond of the diarrhoea either.' He gives a sad smile. Which for some reason makes me feel sad, even though I should be elated. He's clearly bought my story.

'Are you sure that's what you want to do? This aid worker thing?'

'What can I say? It's a dream of mine.' Which is not exactly a lie. I did dream about it once – but it was more a nightmare because I didn't just get diarrhoea, I had big boils and was foaming at the mouth. Watching a Zombie movie just before bed is never a good idea.

'I see. Well, I wouldn't want to stand in the way of anyone's dreams. It makes sense now why you don't really get involved.'

I just nod with wide eyes.

'So, what have you done so far?' Stu leans forward in interest.

'Hmm?'

'Well, I'm assuming you must have done some aid work closer to home already?'

'Oh...yes! Of course! You know, helping the homeless – regular stuff like that.'

I gave a homeless guy my Costa Caramel Latte once, and I've taken heaps and heaps of clothes to the charity shop – some I've only worn once. Not to mention I have a monthly direct debit set up for Oxfam. The money goes towards helping build homes in villages in Africa. It's all helping the homeless one way or another when you really think about it.

'You make me feel bad Gina, I should do more to help those less fortunate than me. Tell me how I can help?'

'Hm?'

'How can I help with some of your causes?'

'Oh! Well...you can...' And as if by some miracle I hear the trill of the Jaws ringtone coming from my bag. I reach in for my phone, look at the number, and hold the phone to my chest.

'I really have to take this, and unfortunately it means I'm going to have to cut our date short. But it was great meeting you!'

I jump off my stool, shake his hand *and* kiss his cheek. I spin on my heel and put the phone to my ear so that Stu doesn't feel obligated to add a few parting words. A few steps out of earshot I finally answer the call.

'No!' I hiss 'No, I don't want a free quote for a new conservatory. I told you people this last week already!'

I press the button to end the call but keep the phone to my ear in case Stu is still looking.

As I make a beeline towards the door, my eyes meet Mr Glass sharer who is now standing near the exit. He smiles cheekily and raises his glass to me, which still has my lipstick imprinted on it. I haughtily lift my chin as I walk past him and end up spinning twice through the revolving exit door (damn it, they always confuse me).

***

'So, how did this one go?' Lisa sounds so excited. That's soon going to change.

'Hmm, I think this maybe is another no no.'

'No way! I can't believe that. He's a bus driver, and you're practically a model! Anyone can do the math with that scenario.' Lisa is using her adamant tone.

'What can I say?'

My friend is silent for a little too long. 'Lisa?'

'What *did* you say?'

'What do you mean what did I say? If I didn't know any better, I'd think from your tone that you were accusing me of something.'

I'm hoping I've got just the right amount of indignant innocence in my voice.

'I'm sorry, but I am finding it very difficult to comprehend why this guy would turn down the chance of a second date with you. No one turns down the chance of a second date with you Gina!'

'Roger did.'

'And I'm *still* trying to figure that one out. You really don't realise how gorgeous you are, do you?' Okay, *that* makes me blush a little. 'And it's not just on the outside either. Someone deserves the chance to appreciate that, and you deserve to be the object of that appreciation. That's why everyone – even Delilah - is so eager to help you find that special someone. Okay, maybe Delilah's reasons are a little different to everyone else's but she's still on the same page. Unless there's some reason, why you want to be by yourself?'

This is the perfect opening. The ideal opportunity to finally tell my best friend my secret.

'Gina? *Is* there something? Some reason?'

Her words bring me back to reality. Which is No Revelations today.

'What reason could there possibly be? Pul-lease.'

'Well, what happened then?'

I can tell my friend is not going to let this rest.

'Well, we spoke for a while, and it was all quite pleasant. And then I told him about what I dreamed of doing and that didn't seem to sit too well with him.'

'You're kidding! What, he doesn't like women who know what they want to do with their life? He'd prefer someone who doesn't want to move forward?'

'Well, when you put it like *that*...' I taper off to let Lisa fill in the blanks with her own imagination. Anyway, moving forward is in the same region as travelling. Planes fly forwards not backwards. It may not be exact, but it's close enough I'd say.

'What a sexist pig! If your dream makes him feel threatened, then sod him. On to the next one!' I can hear Lisa pound the table with her fist.

'Absolutely! When is the next one, by the way?'

In her excitement to tell me what's next in her dating diary for me, she doesn't pick up that I've subtly changed the subject. And just like that, Stu is now old news. It's handy that Lisa has always known my dream is expanding my business, and not correcting her gives me plausible deniability if this ever comes on top. So I'll just leave her to think that while I start thinking about what I can tell the next guy.

Fourteen

I've been on a date every night this week so far since Sunday. At this rate, I'm going to run out of ideas to keep these men at bay, and at the same time, make it look like they're the ones keeping *me* at bay.

The crazy thing is, is that none of them were candidates put forward by the Three Fs. That's my new name for everyone, by the way. Three Fs being Friend, Family and Foe. The Friend being Lisa, The Family, I think that's self-explanatory, and of course, my Foe, who else but the Dreadful Delilah. Lisa was quite impressed when I told her, especially by being the first F. She gave me a high five when I told her about the third F.

Anyway, getting back to the point. It seems that the word has somehow gotten out (from Mum, I'm sure) that I'm more or less dating anyone that will ask dates and guys just seem to be falling out of the woodwork. I really need to get a hold of those business cards with my details on that Mum has been handing out like promotional flyers. The thing is, Lisa has eyes and ears everywhere, not to mention she can be a little tricky – I've not been able to even hint an excuse to get out of these social encounters, just in case she's set one of them up through a third party to try and catch me out. I know she's not entirely convinced I'm on board with this. She even still wants to know about the date even if she didn't have anything to do with arranging it. I'd always tell her anyway, even when I didn't have to – but now instead of talking freely, I have to be creative with what I tell her. Geez, girly gossiping is supposed to be enjoyable.

My stories to put these guys off are really start-ing to evolve. One guy I told I was a practicing White Witchery and could make him a spell to grow back his hair. He seemed more offended than anything else because I believe he thought the four strands he kept rearranging already constituted a full head of hair. The second guy was quite simple. I knew he was a die-hard Arsenal Supporter so I told him I was Tottenham's greatest fan. I even borrowed a Tottenham shirt from Marko. I need to get it back to him because it really is the best thing in his wardrobe.

I really outdid myself when I told the last one I was going to be in an experiment to live without technology for a year and that I needed a partner. When he reached for his phone to help me find one on Facebook, I knew he wasn't putting himself forward. Another score for me on the No-No-for-a-second-date Date-ometer!

'So, another bummer date, huh?' Lisa doesn't sound as surprised as she usually does. I think she may be getting a little suspicious. Even though my stories are getting easier, keeping my secret isn't. Especially from this best friend of mine.

'Yeah. Guess I'm just a little on the unlucky side at the moment.'

'Your Mum said she just happened to pass by the restaurant and saw you deep in conversation with someone that wasn't on my clipboard. She took a picture and Whatsapped it to the group.'

Yes, you heard correctly. The Three Fs have a Whatsapp group to keep updated about my dating escapades.

'I don't know if it was the flash, but his teeth looked kind of bright.'

'No, that wasn't the flash. They really *are* blindingly white.' I squint again just thinking about them. What is it with some of these guys? I'd really thought Mum's candidate Stuart was a one-off. Are they using an Ultra whitening toothpaste that's not on sale to the general public?

'So?'

'So...?'

'Sooo. What happened this time?'

'What, on the date?

'Of course, on the date.' I can hear Lisa's barely contained sarcasm.

'Oh...yeah, we had a good time. He seemed like a nice guy, but you never can really tell, right?'

'I already know the feeling must have been mutual. I don't think I've met a guy who is still breathing that wouldn't give their right arm to date you just once, never mind twice!'

I can feel myself blushing. I need to change the subject.

'Right...right... anyway, how was your day off? Did you go shopping like you planned? What did you get? Anything nic...'

Lisa interrupts 'Ooh, yes I did! I got something great and I'll tell you all about it...after you've told me about the date.'

Damn it, how does she have that uncanny knack of steering a conversation back in the direction *she* wants it to go? I really need to learn how to do that.

'Nothing much to tell really. As I said, we got on really well.'

'So when is date number two? If you let me know now I can make sure it doesn't clash with any of the other dates I have planned for you.' I can hear Lisa rustling paper and I know she's looking at that stupid clipboard again.

'No need to worry about that happening. I don't think I'm going to be seeing him again.' The rustling on the other end of the phone stops. Lisa is quiet for the next ten seconds. About the same amount of time as I'm holding my breath and closing my eyes - waiting for her reaction.

'So. Let me get this straight. You had a nice time. He was a nice guy. You both got on "really well" I believe were your exact words – which in my book is better than "well" on its own. Yet, you don't think you're going to see him again?'

If I know Lisa – and I do know my friend – that is the calm before the storm. I can just never remember whether I'm actually supposed to answer the question or not when she gets like this.

'Erm...yes?'

'I see. That reminds me. You'll never guess who I bumped into yesterday?'

Great! Finally, a change of subject

'Whooo?' I know I shouldn't sound quite so excited, but this feels on the verge of a good old fashioned gossip fest – the type that's still fun.

'Roger.'

'Roger?' Who's Roger I wonder? And what has he been up to, aye?

'Roger, your date who took all your change because his Oyster card was short when he needed to go sign on for his unemployment cheque.'

'Oh...*that* Roger.' Okay. I can hear an alarm bell tinkling a little.

'And you'll never guess what he told me.'

'Hold on...*where* did you bump...'

Lisa talks right over me like I didn't say a word,

'...he told me that you were one of the fittest women he'd ever seen that wasn't on the cover of Playboy and that you told him you had a calling to be a Nun.'

I literally stop breathing. But I can't flake out now.

'Well. All I can say to *that* is anyone who can use Playboy and Nuns in the same sentence...well, need I say more? I *did* tell you he was a little out there. So, you'll never guess who *I* saw the other day in a jogging suit and the highest heels ever!'

'Theresa.'

'No, it was...Yes. It *was* Theresa. How did you...?' How did she...?

'I'm not finished!' Lisa cuts me off again, 'As I was saying, so when Roger told me this, it suddenly made sense why there was no mention of a second date.'

Okay, alarm bells are ringing now, full toll – think Quasi Modo.

'And then I also bumped into Stu. Well, not so much bumped into him as I got his number from your Mum and called him up. You remember Stu, don't you? Bus driver, your Mum's favourite-would-be-son-in-law?'

Well, didn't she just have the clumsiest day bumping into everyone. I'm unsure whether I'm supposed to answer this question, so I stay silent and just listen.

'He too said that you were absolutely gorgeous but he couldn't stand in the way of you wanting to travel the world helping people in diseased countries – which would be commendable if it was true.'

Still just listening...

'So?' Lisa emphasises.

Okay is this still all rhetorical? Or am I actually supposed to answer this time? I'm so confused right now!

'GINA!' My friend shouts down the phone.

'Yes!' I jump and answer immediately.

'What's going on?' Lisa sounds firm.

'I...I...' I don't even know what to say. Even I can't think of a story to get out of this. I am royally screwed right now.

'Don't even THINK of lying to me like you did those guys Virginia Sonia Robbins!'

Okay, when my full birth given name gets called out, it means my friend is mad at me and she isn't going to stop letting me know that any time soon.

'I had a feeling something funny was going on when you told me Roger wasn't into you, but I just brushed it off. I mean, please – he could only dream of meeting someone like you, did you *see* his ponytail? It was like something from a real pony!'

'That's what I thought!'

Lisa doesn't even break a beat as she talks over me.

'But then Stu, too? We're talking Stu? Nice, normal, gets-on-with-mothers Stu? No way two guys in a row don't want a second chance with a chick like you when every other guy since I've known you would break his right arm to be your fella. In fact, remember Vonnie? He actually did!'

'Oh goodness, that was an accident!'

I insisted to Vonnie that I would wait for my Mum to come with the spare key when I locked myself out. How was I to know he would charge into the door shoulder first when I mentioned I thought I'd left the cooker on (which thankfully I hadn't by the way.)

'Whatever! You fabricated those stories to Roger and Stu. You deliberately sabotaged the chance of a second date with them. And I already know the reasons are going to be as dumb as all the other reasons you find to not date.'

'Hey! Barry Galloway having bad breath was not a dumb reason! It made the ends of my hair curl, it was so bad. And when you met him, it made the ends of *your* hair curl!'

I feel quite indignant that she could even forget that.

'Okay, that reason maybe was a good reason, but the rest are just dumb, dumb, *dumb* Gina! We just want to see you with someone special, you *deserve* someone special! You agreed to us helping you, you said you were on board with us setting you up. I just can't begin to understand why you are determined to stay single when half the male population is practically begging to not only take you off the shelf, but to take the shelf as well!'

Lisa is on a roll now. She's not stopping for breath; she is really pissed at me! The more she rants, the more this strange feeling is coming over me. It's the one I felt for a second last week when I was talking to Stu and thought I could tell him what I've never been able to tell anyone. Only this time, the feeling is stronger. It's bubbling up from my stomach and rising into my chest...

'I'm not kidding Gina, you really need to...'

Lisa continues, not stopping for me to get a word in even if I wanted to. The feeling is now in my throat, moving to the tip of my tongue. It's overwhelming. I blurt it out before I can stop myself.

'I've never done it before!'

Lisa stops. I don't know if it's because of what I said or because she really needed to take a breath.

'What? What do you mean you've never done it before? Gone on a second date? Well, what do you expect if you tell them you want to be a Nun? You don't give them a chance to get past date one!

Honestly, it's like riding a bike, it gets easier with practice. Do you remember...'

'No Lisa, I mean I haven't *done* it before.'

Lisa stops again, clearly confused. 'Oh...kay...'

I can almost hear the cogs turning in her mind.

'I give up. What haven't you done before?'

This is the point of no return. As Usher sang - This is my confession.

'*It*, Lisa. I haven't done *it* before. I'm a...still a...virgin.'

Lisa is silent on the other end of the phone. This is a record for even her. It must really be taking a while to sink in. Understandably. Suddenly she laughs.

'I can't believe you are still making up stories! But this is fantastical even for you - stop kidding around!'

Her laughter gradually dies down in the face of my not denying my outburst. She's waiting for me to respond now. To retract my statement. But it's out there now and for the first time, I don't want to take it back. I need to share this, and who better than with my best friend. I still can't believe I managed to get it out without choking. I think it's finally sinking in – for both of us.

'You're serious? You're 35 and never had sex?'

To hear someone else say those words finally gives me back my voice.

'That's right. And now you know why I avoid going on dates, especially second dates because that's when the conversation really starts getting personal.'

'You're 35 years old and never had intercourse? That's what you're saying?'

'Yes. And before you ask me again why I'd make something like that up – think for yourself, why would I make something like that up?'

'You own a sexy lingerie store. You advise all kinds of women what lacy knickers will make their partners pulsate. But you've never worn sexy underwear to make anyone pulsate. That's what you're saying?'

'Erm, yes again. I haven't actually done that. I've just read a lot of historical Mills and Boons and creatively fill in any blanks.'

'Your picture caused one of your Dad's mates to get so worked up, that your Dad punched him out. But you've never gotten anyone worked up like that in person. Like physically. That's what you're saying?'

'Well Norman, you know the gassy guy I went to that new cinema opening with? His intestines went into overdrive when we first met. He said that only ever happens when he meets someone he really likes – it was like a nervous reaction or something. I don't know if that counts as getting someone worked up?'

'You know no-one would believe this right?'

'Yes, I know that.'

'That's your story and you're sticking to it?'

'It's not a story, and yes I am.'

Lisa goes unexpectedly silent after that. The ten seconds that have passed feel like ten minutes – in any case, it's a lot longer than I thought it would be. I can just imagine the initial disbelief gradually sinking in and the look on her face morphing into shock – her eyes opened wide and her mouth fallen open, jaw dropped inviting any passing flies to take residence. Even though she's my best friend, I'm immediately glad that we're not face to face. Suddenly, I hear a loud thud at the other end of the phone which sounds remarkably like the phone receiver hitting the ground.

'Lisa? LISA?'

But instead of Lisa's voice, I hear an even louder thud which if I'm not mistaken, sounds a lot like my best friend hitting the floor in a dead faint.

Fifteen

I spend the next five minutes yelling Lisa's name down the phone and being in a panicked state of whether I should go to her house to make sure she's okay or stay on the phone to make sure she's okay.

'I'm okay! I'm okay! Nobody panic!' Lisa finally shouts down the phone and I don't know whether I'm more relieved that she's conscious again or that I've finally told her my big secret.

'Are you sure? I've been yelling down the phone for ages and it *did* sound like you hit something really hard.'

Like the floor.

'It's just a little bump on the head. I can make the bluey purple colour it's rapidly turning into work with a denim shirt or something. More importantly...you did say what I thought you said, didn't you?'

'Yes. Yes, I did. In all of the versions you thought I was saying it in.'

'Are *you* okay?'

'Yes, why wouldn't I be?'

'Well because...'

'Because what? Because I haven't done it yet?'

'Well...yes.'

'So let me ask you something. I haven't done it yet, so there must be must be something wrong?' I don't know what I expected her to say when everything kicked in, but it wasn't this.

'No! No. Of course I'm not saying there's anything wrong with you – just making sure it wasn't something medically related.'

'No, I'm as fit as a fiddle according to my last doctor's health check.'

'And there's nothing wrong with saving it for religious purposes either. You know, waiting until you're married and stuff.'

'Oh...so there'd be something wrong if it *wasn't* for religious purposes like saving "it" until I was married – is *that* what you're saying then?' My relief is fast turning to agitation.

Lisa sounds carefully calm on the other end of the phone, 'I just don't understand why…I mean how…you know what? Forget everything I've said so far. What I should have said is it must have been a big deal for you to tell me that after keeping it from me for, well, for all the years that I've known you.'

Geez, she's being so understanding and it's making me feel like a giant sized turd.

'I wanted to tell you, Lisa. Years ago, I really did. But it's not like it's something you can just bring up in everyday conversation – like "Hi Lisa, bought some great shoes today, saw a dress that was totally you, and by the way, I'm still a virgin at 35."'

'But that's just it. You so could have brought it up in everyday conversation - because *anything* and everything with us comes under "everyday conversation". So if you didn't know before, you know now. Because if you ever keep something like this from me again; I *will* kick your ass, okay?'

'Okay.' Thankfully this is a kind of unique situation so unlikely there'll be anything even remotely like this to keep secret again. Just the same, I agree quickly without protest. Lisa was a junior black belt at ten years old so I really don't want to call her bluff on this. We're both silent for the next few minutes.

'Right then. I'm gonna pop over and we can talk some more over a cuppa. See you in twenty.'

Ten minutes later, Lisa is ringing my doorbell like her finger is stuck on it. I hope no old ladies, foxes or chickens happened to be crossing the road whilst she was on her way here.

'Okay, peppermint tea bags – check. Butterkist popcorn – check. And we are a go.' Lisa brushes past me with the items in hand, 'Now, I've had a long hard think about – let's call it your *situation*.'

'Erm, you've known about my *situation* for just over ten minutes.'

Lisa waves her hands dismissively at me as if to brush away what I just said.

'...and I don't think this needs to change anything in terms of our dating plan for you.'

I think my friend bumped her head a little harder than she thinks. Even though, she has done a rather good job of matching the colour of the bruise with her shirt.

'No, don't look at me as if I'm crazy – I mean it. This is even more of a reason to find you somebody special.'

Lisa looks like she's had an epiphany, while the only look I can muster is confusion. Lisa is tapping her chin like a person possessed as her mind formulates what I am now confident must be a crazy plan.

'Erm... how did you come to *that* conclusion?' I throw my hands in the air. Now Lisa is pacing up and down and I can almost see a light bulb above her head.

'Okay, I know a crazy plan hatching when I see one. What is going on in that brain of yours?'

'All you need to know right now is that the dating show will go on. In fact, the next Find-you-a-date meeting is tomorrow, so that doesn't give me much time...need to re-think...make a few adjustments to the calendar on the clip board...'

She suddenly grabs her jacket and makes towards the front door.

'Hey, where are you going? You just got here! What happened to talking over tea?'

'I know and we *will* talk more about this – don't think that we won't, but right now I have to prepare for tomorrow's meeting. We are going to kill two birds with one stone – find you a fella and lose you your virginity!'

I don't hide my look of apprehension at this point.

'Don't worry, it will all become clear tomorrow. And Gina? Thanks for telling me.'

I sense the hurt she's trying not to show and right now I feel like the first time I wore thongs – really uncomfortable. I know I'd be just as hurt if she kept something like this from me. Luckily, if Lisa gets a pimple on her arse, she can't keep it to herself. And that's the one topic that I actually wish she would.

'You know I'm *itching* to hear the *whole* story, don't you? I mean it's like a Hollywood storyline - how someone who looks like you has managed to hang onto something like that for this long. But...' Lisa reaches for my hand and gives it a big squeeze, 'I figure just telling me after all this time is a big enough step for one night. So. To be continued.'

She starts to walk towards the door again, then suddenly swings round and envelopes me in the tightest biggest bear hug – which lasts silently for a few minutes before she shoots through the door leaving me with just the echo of a loud slam.

Sixteen

'Okay everyone, let's get this show on the road. Who's next to put forward their date candidate?'

Lisa really doesn't believe in beating around the bush. And today, neither do I. I just want her to get straight to the part that she prepared last night after she rushed off. However, if rushing this process means there's a possibility of our last conversation going further than her ears, then I will happily wait impatiently.

'I believe that would be me.' Cousin Mona has actually put away her smart phone – well it's not so much put away as it is resting on the table in front of her. It's normally stuck to her hand like a sixth finger. She actually seems quite eager to put forward her candidate.

Lisa looks up from her clip board, 'Great Mona, we're all ears.'

As I look around the room, they really *are* all ears. In fact, this looks like it's turned into some type of occasion. Mum is serving everyone her home made Victoria sponge and Gran is pouring everyone tea. Even Delilah is looking a little more dressed up than usual – I've never thought of a body con dress as casual attire.

'His name is Gregory Corbett. He's a lecturer at my University and is really intelligent,'

She mentions intelligence as if it's a qualification. And here I was thinking intelligence was a given for a teacher.

'I think he'd make a great date for my Cuz and if all goes well, he'll no doubt feel obliged to be generous with his girlfriend's cousin's assignment marks – so added bonus!' Cousin Mona quickly replaces her big grin with an innocent look, 'Oh, did I forget to mention that he teaches Nutritional Science which I am a little too close for comfort to failing?'

I would likely fail it too. Probably because I didn't even know there was a science to nutrition. Mum, on the other hand, is beaming.

'Ooh, it would be so nice to have a teacher in the family. I still haven't quite got the knack of flaky pastry. He'd be able to teach me the science behind the recipe when he comes round for dinner.'

Hello? I've not even met the guy yet and he's gone from boyfriend to family member in the space of two sentences.

'Can I just put it out there that it's just a date. Just the very *first* date.' I feel compelled to remind them.

'Of course, dear.' Mum answers. But already I can see the cogs of her mind formulating questions to ask him like why is a carrot more orange than an orange? And is green pasta healthier for you than white? I look over at Dad – my usual last haven of sanity – to be rescued, but he's borrowed my phone and his full concentration right now is on a game of Candy Crush.

'Anyway, I told him I had a single cousin who was hot and ran a lingerie store. He didn't seem to need any more information after that.'

'Great! So when is he available?' Lisa is business-as-usual. I wonder if she's forgotten what I told her last night? I immediately dismiss the thought. It's not exactly forgettable news, now is it?

'He said whenever Gina was available, he would be too and to just give him 24 hours notice.'

'Great! So text him now and tell him it'll be tomorrow at 7.00pm at Rymans Bar.'

'Seriously Lisa?' I look over at my friend.

'Why wait?' She gives me a stare, 'He's ready, you're ready...'

Okay, I know what she's trying to tell me with that coded look. And no, I'm not ready for *that*.

'What I'm saying is, that's where I went for the date with Stu.' I give her back a hard same-coded stare. 'What if I bump into him?'

'No chance of that, he told your mother he was doing some extra night shifts on the buses.'

'Yes dear,' Mum adds 'He's saving up for a van so that he can do private drop-offs for the elderly at the weekends. Such an ambitious boy.' Mum sighs and raises an eyebrow at me suspiciously. I know she thinks it's my fault that me and Stu didn't work out – which technically I guess it is. Luckily he's too much of a gentleman to confirm that to her. I reckon even if it wasn't my fault, she'd still find a way to side with her wanna-have son-in-law. It's a shame how it all worked out, as he really was a nice guy. In another life, he might potentially have been the one – for Mum *and* for me. Lisa waves a coupon in the air.

'Plus, I managed to blag a double happy hour voucher with two free snacks in exchange for you giving Mags the owner a discount on a set from your Dark Spice range.' Lisa gives a wink.

'What if I'm not available for double happy hour?' Does no-one think to ask me anything about my own time anymore?

'You're forgetting again, Virginia.' My Gran waves my personal Diary *and* my work diary in the air. Actually, is that my work diary? I'm sure my work diary is red while that one is blue? I squint my eyes to get a better look.

'It just made sense to just copy the details into a different diary Virginia – you can have this one afterwards. It's a much nicer colour than that tatty red one you've got.'

Okay, that's officially taken running my life to another level.

'I've given that tatty one back to Patsy by the way. You know, in case there are new bookings to add in the meantime.' Gran lovingly strokes the blue diary. I don't even bother to comment on what a gross invasion of my privacy this all is – that horse has already bolted. I just want to get to the part of this meeting where everything is supposed to become clear like Lisa said it would last night before she left.

'Okay everyone, I think that's a wrap for tonight. Don't forget you can get me by phone, text, email, Whatsapp, Facebook, Twitter, Instagram, and for you Mr Shah – Linked In.' Lisa rests her clipboard on top of the TV and does a wide stretch of her arms.

Everyone starts rising, getting coats, putting away teapots. I jump up and grab Lisa's arm.

'Erm...still not *clearer*!'

'Right, I haven't explained yet have I?' Lisa looks over her shoulder to make sure no one can overhear and draws me close to the window.

'Now, before I go into it and you go into one, just hear me out okay? This is all just based on theory but it's a sound theory. I thought about it all night.'

'Oh...kay' I answer cautiously.

'So firstly, what's happened when you've told people about your situation in the past?'

'What do you mean?'

'I mean how have people responded when you've told them?'

'I haven't.'

'You haven't what?'

'I haven't told anyone.'

'Okay, I'm not talking about recently, I mean before.'

'I haven't told anyone before.'

Lisa is looking perplexed, like she can't quite get what I'm saying.

'What? Like not ever?'

'Yes. Not ever. Except you.'

'Really? I'm the only person you've told? Ever, ever?' Lisa's eyes open wide, and I'm sure she's trying to hold back a smile.

'That's correct. Ever, ever. So now we've cleared that up, what's this theory? I have a date in less than 24 hours, so spilling the beans any time now would be great.'

I don't know why I feel so on edge. Like this theory of Lisa's will change my world or something. I reach for the unfinished bag of Butterkist popcorn that Lisa bought yesterday. Popcorn just makes things seem better somehow. I think it might be the soothing crunch of them.

'Yes, right! Okay, what I was thinking is that as you've waited such a long time to get this big secret off your chest – or should I say lower – that the best way to handle this is to actually...literally...just do it again.'

'Do...what again?'

She cannot be saying what I think she's saying. Because I think she's saying that I should tell my secret again, but she simply cannot be saying that.

'Tell that you're a...virgin?' Lisa closes her eyes and braces herself for my reaction. I sort of go into a trance as her statement washes over me. My imagination goes into overdrive and suddenly I'm transported to a news conference held in what looks like the local gym hall where I'm going to do what Lisa suggested - tell everyone my secret...

I'll admit I'm a little nervous standing on this news pulpit surrounded by reporters. I see all the most popular news outlets for Mapledene Road are in full attendance to hear my special announcement.

Mrs Robbins – or Mum - from the Evening Round Up is front row with a plate of lemon drizzle cupcakes held high for all to sample.

Mr Robbins – or Dad - from the Sunday Sport is just behind her, looking at his watch every few seconds. I forgot Golfing Masters will be on soon. I'll make a note to wrap this up ASAP, that way he'll only miss maybe the first ten minutes.

Even Cousin Mona from *The Student Lounge* has made it, and is using a Dictation app on her phone to record my mysterious message, whilst reaching for one of her Aunt's cupcakes. I hope there are some left over; I could do with a cupcake right now to calm my nerves.

Mr Shah from *Business Today* is sitting with what looks like several co-reporters who all have an uncanny resemblance to one another.

Lisa from *The Organiser* is also front row with her clip board sitting next to Mum, primarily to get easy access to the cupcakes. It's an industry worst-kept secret that she has a weakness for lemon cake. She gives me a thumbs up for encouragement. I should think so too, this is all her theoretical idea after all.

I already anticipated Delilah from the B.I.T.C.H (Beauty, In-style, Technique, Clothes & Hair) sup-plement of *Every Woman* wouldn't miss this. She is also at the front using FaceTime on her iPad as a live feed.

My Gran – who I'll just refer to as my Gran – is representing *Genteel Times* and sipping tea, patiently waiting to hear what I've got to say.

Patsy, my assistant from *Art of Lingerie* is bob-bing around at the back of the room on her seat *when she should be changing the stock in the shop window. She gives me a big smile and wave of excitement.*

There are a few others I don't recognise, which is to be expected. My news is going to be BIG.

I cough to get everyone's attention.

'Hello everyone. Thank you all for coming today. I'm just going to get straight to the point. This is something I've only recently felt able to share in light of your efforts to help me meet a special someone – so to speak. So here it is...my announcement...that I've called you all here for...' I know I'm rambling now but I can't seem to get the words out. I look over to Lisa who mouths at me 'Go on, you can do it.'

That's enough for me to quickly say quietly, 'I'm a Virgin.'

'Sorry, what was that dear? I didn't quite catch that?' Mum says as she circles the room, making sure everyone has a cupcake including the security guard.

I take a deep breath and say louder, 'I'm a Virgin. I've never had sex.'

The room suddenly goes deathly silent – you could hear a pin drop. This is soon shattered by a broken clatter as Mum spins round and drops the plate of cupcakes.

Gran drops her cup of tea, spilling some onto Dad's lap.

Dad drops his jaw both due to the hot tea and the even hotter news he's just heard.

Patsy drops on her arse as she falls off her seat.

Cousin Mona drops her phone – but luckily catches it before it hits the ground.

Delilah drops the cupcake she just took from Mum.

Lisa is looking from left to right, right to left just trying to take everyone's reactions in.

Then mayhem breaks out, as if the pin drop just turned into a bomb explosion! Camera flashes from smart phones are going off in my face from all directions.

Delilah recovers first and shoots her hand in the air to ask the first question, 'Do you have one? A vagina?'

Mum recovers second to swing round to face her indignantly, 'Of course she does! Since she was a baby!' She then turns to face me, 'Has it stopped working dear? Have you seen Doctor Mills?'

Suddenly, everyone is firing questions at me!

'You'll be compared to a Yeti or the Loch Ness monster as something people never thought existed – a 35-year-old virgin. How do you feel about that?'

'Are you allergic to sex?'

'Can I have your autograph?'

Gran quickly comes over to give me a hug and stroke my hair, saying 'There, there Virginia, it'll be okay. Genteel Times wouldn't publish such a thing. On the other hand, you might be offered a windfall payment from a tacky tabloid for an exclusive!'

Dad is cursing, 'Who traumatised my little girl?' and looking around like he wants to punch someone.

Cousin Mona is tweeting: My cousin – Virginia by name, Virgin by nature #student lounge

Delilah is holding up her iPad with an evil grin, using the camera to film me, 'This will be the perfect clip for a new series pitch Sex-less in the City! B.I. T.C.H will promote me to interviewing for D.E.V. I.L after this (DoItYourself Entrepreneurs who are Vulnerable In Love).'

Lisa is trying to calm everyone down. The security guard comes over to me, gives me a big wink and whispers in my ear, 'I can help you with that little problem...'

The questions are coming from every angle – I can't even distinguish what they are asking. Every-

one is walking towards me at the same time, all talking at the same time, all snapping their smart phone cameras at me at the same time. I'm backing away as they get closer and closer while the room starts spinning faster and faster...

I snap out of my trance and whirl round towards Lisa.

'Are you high? I can't just tell everyone! I've only just about told you after nearly twenty years! Can you imagine me telling my Mum? Or my Dad? Or, heaven forbid – *Delilah?* Well I can imagine, and it's not pretty!'

I can hear the panic rising in my voice. I'm starting to hyperventilate. Lisa rushes over to me and grabs the bag of popcorn out of my hand and empties the contents into the empty teapot that hasn't quite made it back to the kitchen yet.

'Breathe Gina, breathe!' She thrusts the empty bag at me to breathe into. I am inhaling all the toffee-ness inside – in out, in out – looking over the top of the bag at her trying to calm down. After a few giant inhales, I feel I can string a sentence together again.

'Lisa, I thought you understood? The whole problem is I can't tell anyone else. That bump you got on your head? It dislodged something. You are now officially nuts if you think *that's* going to happen!"

'Just hear me out. We can find a way for you to tell...'

'No way!'

'But listen...'

'No how!'

'Just wait...'

'Nuh uh!'

'*Listen* for just one minute! You're embarrassed to tell people because of what you *think* their reaction might be, right?'

'It's what I *know* their reaction will be, so...'

'Well, how do you actually know? You said you haven't ever told anyone.'

I start to protest her point, but I can't really. She is technically right, damn her.

'Exactly. So, what if we find a way to help you deal with whatever reaction so you won't feel totally embarrassed? Telling your story again might not be so terrible then, right?'

'Are you kidding me?' I look at my friend in amazement, 'You say that as if it is so simple and straightforward and logical. This isn't something that's logical! A 35-year-old virgin in the middle of London isn't logical! If the powers that be thought this was catching, they would shoot me!

'Don't be silly, no they wouldn't!'

'That's because I've kept it a secret! This is not Sharing is Caring like a can of Coke!'

Lisa is trying to find another way to rephrase her statement while I start breathing into the Butterkist bag again.

'Look, all I'm saying is that you've probably been working yourself up every time for a reaction you might not even get. I mean, did I go all kooky when you told me?'

'Erm, I think passing out and nearly cracking your head open passes for kooky.'

Lisa brushes my statement aside, 'You know what I mean. I'm not saying you have to tell everybody, just the people that immediately count – which are the guys you're going to be dating. All you need to do is test their reactions beforehand. If they get all melodramatic about it, you can tell them you were kidding – they'll laugh it off and at the end of the date you never have to see them again. We can then skip to the next "mature" guy on the list who would be proud to know that he'll be the first to pop the cherry on a chick like you.'

I open my mouth to object and then I stop and think. Could something so stupidly simple really work? It would almost be like playing Gotcha! In fact, it *would* be playing Gotcha!

'You can see it can't you? You know it can work Gina! This is the only thing that's standing in the way of you and your Mr Right. This is how we can bull doze that obstacle.'

I close my thighs and cringe instinctively at her choice of words – whilst at the same time, I think I might actually agree with her. It's a hurdle and if I can jump over it and get my 'cherry popped' as Lisa so eloquently put it, then I will finally be able to move past this. I can't believe what I'm going to say.

'Okay. Let's test your theory on my next date. Tomorrow's date with the university teacher guy.'

'Girl, I'm already way ahead of you.' Lisa jets across the room to get her clip board off the TV, 'here is something I prepared earlier...'

And with that, she starts to explain in detail exactly what she was up to all last night.

Seventeen

'The first time is always the hardest. It gets easier afterwards. For "that" *and* for this.' Lisa is fixing my collar as if it's my first day of school. I keep saying to myself that my friend is wise – she isn't a virgin so she must know what she's talking about.

'So, why doesn't the prospect of telling a second person who happens to be a teacher and also likely a sensible worldly individual – feel easier? I mean is sweating palms a sign of feeling easier? Because I've got to say, it's not the sign of feeling easier I was expecting.'

I'm babbling. Another sign of not feeling easier. Telling Lisa my secret and telling some random teacher my secret? Akin to apples and oranges. In fact, apples and melons. Huge genetically modified super-sized melons versus teeny tiny mini apples. Completely incomparable!

'It's going to be fine. Just stick to the plan. So, have we got the script all memorised?' Lisa looks as nervous as I feel. We've kind of rehearsed a Q and A session to work out if my next date will be a dick or a darling when I confess my sexual non-existence to him.

'I think so.' I take a deep breath.

'It's going to be fine, Gina, it really is.'

And yet, with an hour to go before I put this plan into action, it doesn't feel like that.

'Easy for you to say, you're not the one who has to tell a complete stranger the most embarrassing secret of the century.'

'He's hardly a complete stranger, Gina. He's been one of Mona's lecturers for a whole year.'

'Well, I'm not one of his students and it's not Cousin Mona going on this date.' My feet couldn't get any colder than they are right now.

'You can do this Gina.' It's like Lisa can read my mind. She puts both hands on my shoulders and stares unflinchingly into my eyes,

'You. *Can*. Do. This.'

I take another deep breath, shake my hands, stamp my feet and roll my head around my shoulders a couple of times.

'Okay, last minute go over,' Lisa slaps her ruler in her hand and starts pacing like a drill sergeant, 'what indicators do you look for if he asks that key question – why are you single?'

Eighteen

I am waiting outside Rymans Bar. It's 6.45pm so I'm a little early, I'm agitated and it's bloody freezing. Good old English weather – you can always count on it to be hot as hell one day then like the ice cap the next – no matter what the weather man says, which incidentally was to bring an umbrella, when the advice should have been sheepskin gloves.

You would think stamping my feet and rubbing my hands together to keep out the cold would distract me from the events ahead but it's not. I keep taking deep breaths to calm me but all my lungs are receiving is the second-hand smoke from these two girls beside me.

One of them has teeth that are chattering so much I'm surprised her lips can stay together long enough to smoke the cigarette. The other one – in a rather nice blue dress I might add – is moving her head towards the cigarette rather than bringing the cigarette to her mouth. Her hand is shaking so much from the cold that she can barely keep grip of the thing. I'd forgotten how determined smokers can be.

Okay, now that brief observation is over I'm back to being agitated again. I know I could wait inside the bar, but that didn't go too well last time with the humming and the drinking of someone else's drink. Yet, with every second that goes by with me waiting in this frosty breeze, I am reminded that I do not have the determination of a smoker to brave this weather.

I push the revolving door slowly – no need to twirl in it more times than necessary to get in like the last time when I wanted to get out. I quickly scan the bar from beside one of the pillars near the access doors. I know that Stu is supposed to be working today, but better safe than sorry. I walk to the side of the bar opposite where I sat last time, and this time, I order a drink straight away.

'Glass of red...'

'Here you go Ma'am.' The bar tender lays a glass of white wine before me with a big smile.

'But I haven't...?'

'From the gentleman next to you.'

I look beside me to be greeted with a salute from Glass-sharer guy. I was so busy looking into every far corner of the bar that I didn't even realise I'd sat down next to the same guy as before. I groan inside.

'I just thought I'd get you your own drink from the start.'

It's then I realise that I didn't actually apologise for sipping his drink before. And he seems so smug, that I don't think I'll apologise now either.

'It was a harmless little sip.' I roll my eyes and turn my chair reaching for the glass. The wine is already poured so there's no point in wasting it.

'Yes, and we're practically friends anyway. I mean here you are helping yourself to my drink again even though you have your own.'

I splutter the drink up as I realise I've picked up his glass of red wine instead of my glass of white. Damn my partiality to red wine! I groan to myself again and push his glass towards him. My staunch reluctance to apologise before is replaced with acute embarrassment. I hope this isn't a sign of how my evening is going to progress.

'Sorry.' I gruffly apologise, 'Still, sharing a drink hardly makes us friends.'

'Maybe not one drink, but this is our second shared drink and our third time meeting. I would say that we've at least graduated to acquaintance status.'

I screw my eyes up and turn to stare at him again.

'Third time meeting?' Before I can continue, the bar tender places another glass of wine in front of me – red this time.

'On the house.' He toggles his eyebrows twice at me and licks his lips slowly before serving another customer. I lean back in my seat a little and look at his retreating back. I hear a chuckle next to me and turn to see Glass-sharer guy laughing into his glass of wine. I ignore his laughter.

'As I was saying, I believe you're mistaken. I believe our encounters have been limited to the last one and this.'

'And the one when I came into your shop to change my lingerie order for my...ahem...my cousin. Art of Lingerie, right? Your assistant – Patsy? She usually tends to my needs,' he pauses to look at me and I feel my stupid cheeks flushing a little, 'but you were manning the tills on this occasion.'

I wrack my brains trying to remember. For goodness sakes, it's not as if I work the tills every day. Plus, he isn't exactly hard on the eyes – it's not an instantly-forgettable average face.

'David,' he put out a hand to shake mine, 'my friends call me Dave.'

Suddenly, it hits me.

'Oh...you came in with a red baseball cap and huge dark sunglasses. You're the Dave who orders women's underwear every week?' I point at him accusingly and notice that everyone around the bar has gone quiet and is staring at Dave who doesn't even seem fazed.

'Women like to feel special and I like to feel special women. Sexy underwear works for everyone. Buy some today at Art of Lingerie.' He smiles at the eavesdropping crowd and salutes them with his wine glass and gives me a wink.

The woman in front of me grabs a pencil from the pocket of a passing waiter to scribble down the name of the shop and the man on the other side of me opens up Safari on his iPhone to google it. A few seconds later, I'm tapped on the arm. As I turn around, a flash goes off in my face where a young girl has taken a selfie with me and whispers to her friend 'I think she's a famous knicker designer!'

'That should be a few more customers darkening your shop doors. You're welcome by the way.' Dave does a little head bow. I'm at a bit of a loss for words. So to hide it, I just gulp down my wine – making sure that it is *my* wine this time.

'So, is this your local haunt then?' He asks

'What do you mean?'

'Well, I've seen you drinking here a couple times this week.'

'Oh...yes. I've been having a few ...shall we say meetings of late. Rymans just seems like a convenient spot. I'm meeting someone again this evening actually.'

'It wouldn't happen to be that guy with the glasses over there would it?'

I look to where he is pointing and see a guy of about my height holding an airport type sign so big it could easily be mistaken for a poster. It has my name emblazoned on it in huge capitals. Geez, as if carnations weren't bad enough. I slide off my bar stool, smooth down my skirt and smooth back my hair.

'Yes.' Is all I can muster before walking off straight-backed and flush-faced. The bar tender waves for my attention and slips me a card and a wink. I sigh to myself. All this in less than fifteen minutes – suddenly, nerves are the last thing on my mind.

Nineteen

I walk over to Gregory who is pointing to the sign and showing a picture to people as they leave the bar. Okay, I know the bar is busy, but come on.

'Hey, Gregory. I'm Gina.' I go to shake his hand, and he looks at me suspiciously.

'Erm, I'm who you're looking for?'

He looks at the picture which is on the back of a business card, then at me, then at the picture and then visibly relaxes.

'Sorry. You can't be too careful these days.' He vigorously shakes my hand and then just stands there staring at me.

'Is everything okay?'

'Sorry. Your picture doesn't do you justice.' He's now shifting from one foot to the other. It's a nice feeling to know I'm not the only one who came here with nerves. Of course, it's highly unlikely that his nerves are for the same reason as mine, but what the hey.

'So, shall we find a table? The restaurant area is over there.' I point to the food corner. Gregory indicates that I should lead the way.

As I walk towards the restaurant, I literally don't have to brush past anyone as all the guys are smiling and making a path for me. I look suspiciously at them as I walk slowly by - do I smell or something? Or maybe Gregory does? One guy tips his hat off to me. Right, now that has to be a signal of some sort. I'm not sure why he's signalling me but I tap my nose twice and nod in response. I mean, that's what you do when you get a secret signal isn't it? I just hope I'm not agreeing to something strange – like picking up a mysterious package. Okay, I think I need to stop watching spy movies just before bed.

The waiter in the area seems to have been expecting us – I see him shove what looks very much like the same business card with my picture on that Gregory was showing around earlier. Note to self – ask Mum if randomly giving out business cards with pictures of me is really necessary. The waiter leads us to a table with a reserved sign on it. He hands me two menus as Gregory pulls out my chair. I automatically think this guy is a gentleman and that is not a good start – in that order.

I pass one of the menus over and we both study them in silence. Five minutes pass and we still haven't said anything to each other. It's just starting to feel weird when the waiter appears with his pencil.

'Are you ready to order yet?' The waiter looks at me as if Gregory isn't there. Going by the old adage of ladies first I guess.

'Erm...I think I'll start with the shrimp.'

'Really?' Gregory looks over his menu at me. I've only just noticed that he has quite beady looking eyes. Or it could just be his rather large glasses that make them look that way.

'Why? Isn't the shrimp any good here?' I joke.

'Is the shrimp good anywhere? Did you know that they are regarded as scavengers of the sea?'

'Scav of the what?' I look at the waiter who looks as alarmed as me.

'They are known as bottom dwellers – they feed on parasites at the bottom of the sea. Which means if you eat them, you are also feeding on those parasites.' Gregory resumes looking at his menu again.

'Oh...kay. Maybe I'll try the mini tuna steak.'

'Hmm, are you sure?' Gregory looks over his menu again.

'What's wrong with tuna?' I ask. Even the waiter has drawn up a seat next to me in fascination.

'Well, Tuna bio accumulates Mercury.' He makes a face at me that asks why don't I know this.

'How about bread?' I ask Gregory rather than the waiter, who hasn't bothered to write it down lest he needs to cross it out like my last two choices.

'One word. Gluten.' This time he doesn't even look up from his menu.

'Soup?' Both the waiter and I both cross our fingers.

'Vegetable?' Gregory looks suspiciously at us both.

'Ye...es?' I say slowly.

'Great choice! I'll have the same.' Gregory nods vigorously and hands his menu back to the waiter. I sigh with relief and the waiter clenches his fist and draws it towards himself in triumph before striking a haughty pose and walking off to tend to our order.

'So, nutritional science. Who'd have guessed.' I try to keep the irony out of my voice.

'Yes, finished my doctorate around five years ago, and have been teaching it ever since.'

'So what exactly *is* nutritional science?' As soon as the question pops out, I know I should have tried harder to keep it in. Gregory pushes up his spectacles and goes into a monologue of proteins, carbs, and trans fatty acids. Ten minutes later, he shows no sign of abating and I am literally willing the waiter to return as my constant smile is starting to hurt my face. My prayer is soon answered when as if from nowhere, the waiter appears with two steaming bowls of veggie soup.

'Your cousin Mona is a very bright student, but she really needs to focus on non-digestible fibre and fat soluble vitamins. In fact, we could all focus on it a little more – and be healthier for it.' Gregory accentuates his point by taking a spoonful of soup – with the loudest slurp I ever heard. I sip a spoonful silently. Gregory looks expectantly at me.

'Is something wrong with the soup?' I ask with my spoon mid-air.

'More like something wrong with the way you are eating it.'

My spoon is still mid-air because I can't believe what he's just said, especially as he's the one lapping his soup like a hound. But instead of saying this (part of my amended agreement with Lisa after Roger and Stu, is that I can't do or say anything that might deliberately jeopardise my dates), I cock my head to the side questioningly.

'In Japan, it is considered polite to eat soup loud enough for the chef to hear. It shows that you are eating the food and therefore enjoying it.' He looks expectantly at me again. He surely can not be expecting me to…to slurp my soup too? He nods towards my spoon, which I put in my mouth, close my eyes and…slurp. I can see an older couple in the corner frowning at me. Like I haven't got enough embarrassment to look forward to, without this added on top.

'Geez, isn't soup filling!' I push away my bowl after one spoonful and rub my stomach.

'But you've only had one spoonful?'

'One spoonful too many, you're right!' I laugh, 'but I'm sure by the time you've finished I'll be ready for the main.' There's no way I'm going to slurp my way through the starter. Gregory shrugs and continues slurping his soup.

There's a family on a table two rows away who can't stop staring in our direction. That's no doubt down to the fact that their son has started slurping his soup too and they know he didn't pick that little habit up at home. He's grinning away as he does it. Mummy and Daddy look at one another, shrug and join in. The man on the table next to them also cautiously starts to slurp his soup, as does the couple next to him.

It's not long before everyone who has soup is slurping away in out-of-tune sync, smiling at one another and toasting with their spoons like they are all long lost friends. Gregory seems oblivious to it all and is now slurping in time to the tune in the background – Survivor by Destiny's Child. I'm thinking how appropriate because that's what I'll be if I can get through this first course.

Suddenly, everyone else slurping soup follows suit and now I'm looking around for a hidden camera because this has to be a joke. I would not put something like this past Lisa – she'll think it would help to break the ice, I think it will help me want to break her neck. By now, someone should have jumped out with a camera on their shoulder or a microphone in their hand – that hasn't happened so this really is for real!

All the soup slurpers finish to a round of applause from the waiting staff, one of whom is filming it with his smart phone. The older couple in the corner shake their heads, clearly not feeling entertained in the same way. Gregory pushes his bowl away after scraping the last vestiges of liquid from it.

'That really was a good choice for the starter. I'm quite looking forward to the main now.' Me too, because I'm hoping it will be a *lot* quieter.

'So, Gina. Mona says you have your own business?' Gregory peers through his spectacles making his eyes seem even beadier.

'Yes, I own a lingerie store.'

Gregory's eyes open a little wider as I say that.

'Yes, I believe Mona mentioned that. How interesting. Did you know that edible underwear isn't particularly nutritional but quite tasty?' Gregory coughs, 'I mean I've *heard* they are quite tasty. Does your store sell them?'

'Err...no, I didn't know that. And no, I don't sell them.'

'Oh.' Gregory tries to hide his disappointment. We're both silent for the next few moments.

'Sooo. Nutritional science.' I nod as I say this to Gregory again.

'Are you ready for your main now?' The waiter suddenly appears at my side like a genie with perfect timing and hands me a menu again.

'Erm...could I have a menu please?' Gregory stretches his hand out to the waiter. The waiter peers down his nose at him and practically shoves the menu in his hand before turning back to me with a huge smile.

'I will be back for your order in a few minutes. Take your time.' He then picks up my hand and gives it a gentle kiss before disappearing without so much as glancing at Gregory again.

'You must get that a lot.' Gregory is peering over his glasses again. I've decided it's *not* the glasses making his eyes look so beady. They are simply beady looking eyes.

'Waiters kissing my hand? No, not really. It must be part of the service.'

'No, I think it's part of the service to you. I'm a nutritional scientist, I can sense these things.' I think really? Because I can't see the correlation.

'Oh...kay.'

'Can I ask you a personal question?'

Oh no, here it comes. The dreaded question. I suddenly feel panicked. Everything that I'd rehearsed yesterday with Lisa is all jumbled. I don't know if I can do this.

'Sure you can. But can I just pop to the loo first? Great!' I jump out of my seat before Gregory can respond and make a beeline towards the exit.

'The toilets are that way!' I can hear Gregory shout behind me but I pretend not to hear him. As soon as I'm out of sight I reach for my phone. The phone number I call only rings once.

'So? How's it going?' Lisa sounds as anxious as I feel.

'I can't do it.'

'You can. Like we practised. Just do it.'

'What if...'

'Just do it.'

'How can...'

'Do it!'

'But...'

'DO IT!!' Lisa is shouting now.

'FINE!' I shout back. A couple walks past and give me a concerned look. I smile, do a loco imitation with my finger and point to the phone.

'Call me back straight after, okay?'

'Okay.' And that was it, pep talk over. I decide to really pop to the loo before going back into the restaurant. I walk back in the direction of the restaurant area. Gregory gives me a surprised look as I walk straight past our table and wave my fingers to indicate I'll be two minutes.

The toilet feels almost like a sanctuary that I can bask in for a few moments. I stare at myself in the mirror and reflect on my brief conversation with Lisa. I wish I had as much confidence in myself to answer this guy's questions truthfully without throwing up, as she does. As I top up my mascara, two young girls push through the door and smile at me before continuing their own conversation.

'So Tina, what did you tell him?'

Tina blushes, 'I told him I wasn't ready. Do you think that was the wrong thing to do, Candy?'

Candy pulls down what's either the shortest dress or the longest top I've ever seen.

'Well, he is totally hot Tina, and he's into you. He's not the kind of guy to wait around.'

'I know, but it's only been the second date. I think we should wait at least until date four for my first time.' Tina roots around in her purse and pulls out some lipstick.

'You didn't tell him that it would be your first time did you, Tina? He'll think you're a freak for not doing it yet – you *are* twenty one.' Candy folds her arms and looks at her friend. I, on the other hand, am barely managing to hold my tongue.

'No! I couldn't. I was way too embarrassed.' Tina starts powdering her nose.

Candy smears on some of her friend's lipstick, which is actually a really good match for her dress/top and puckers up in the mirror, 'If you ask me, I'd say it's not a big deal, so just do it already.'

I swirl around to face them. The ship where I should mind my own business has now sailed.

'I'm sorry to butt in...no, actually I'm not sorry. Tina...may I call you Tina?' I don't stop for her to give me permission, 'Let me congratulate you for sticking to your guns and not letting this guy rush you to do on date two what you are rightly entitled to wait to do until date four. Or even date six! This is a precious gift you have and you want to entrust it to someone who is going to appreciate waiting for it.'

Both girls, look at each other and then at me. I am now standing with my hands on my hips.

'What you have achieved – and yes, it is an achievement because as you know, there aren't many of us...I mean many *women* who manage to preserve "that" for someone who deserves it rather than give it up to some random guy just because he's hot or because you never thought the cutest boy in school would ever look at someone like you.' I look pointedly at Candy who now looks suitably contrite.

'You shouldn't be embarrassed,' I wag my finger at her, 'you should be proud!'

I lift my chin up to the sky, 'you could start a blog to reach out to all those other twenty-something, and even thirty –something aged women out there who still haven't done the do.'

'Wow...do you really think there are women in their thirties that haven't done it yet too?' Tina looks at Candy who looks at Tina, both jaws looking like fly traps. I click my fingers to get their attention.

'Ahem...the *point* is we...I mean you, may not know many others like you, but trust me when I say you are *not* the only one in that situation who is over twenty!' I start to pace up and down the toilet walkway, waving my purse for emphasis, 'you, Tina, yes *you,* could be their beacon of hope, their reason to wave the "V" flag saying Pride, not Pressure!'

Both girls start to clap rapturously, 'You are *so* right!' Tina clicks her fingers in a zig zag, and moves her head from side to side, 'If Mr Too-Hot can't wait until date four, or even date six, then he can just jog on!'

'I'm so sorry for saying it's not a big deal, Tina.' Candy gives her friend a big hug, 'Do you think there's any way I could get mine back?'

'Well, did it go *all* the way in...?'

As the two girls fix each others hair and discuss how Candy can – so to speak – "put the genie back in the bottle", I take this moment to sneak out of the bathroom. I lean against the door and take a deep breath before going back to the restaurant. You know what? I *can* do this. Just like I told Tina, this is nothing to be ashamed of.

Twenty

Gregory sort of semi stands when I arrive back.

'There are some private toilets that way that not too many people know about, but when I got there, there was a queue.' I pre-empt his question of why did I go in the opposite direction to the large gold arrow pointing at an even larger toilet sign.

'Not many people know about it...but there was a queue?' He pushes his glasses up to stare at me in confusion.

'That's exactly what I thought! Go figure.' Before I get a chance to draw out my chair, the waiter magically appears again and does it for me with a flourish. I smile my thanks, pick up the menu and concentrate on the food options calmly, yet like my life depends on it. Gregory after a few more seconds seems to accept my explanation with a shrug of his shoulders and goes back to looking at his menu. Unsure on what to choose after my earlier schooling in starters, I sneak an apprehensive look over him to see if he's concentrating on his choice enough to not be bothered with mine. I look at the waiter who nods encouragingly at me that this could be my moment to get my choice in there. I give a little cough.

'I wonder what the pasta is like?' I say thoughtfully to the waiter. Gregory doesn't even look up from his menu to say, 'Pasta, especially white pasta can be bloating if you're not careful,' and as if to emphasise, he adds, 'and we all know what goes hand in hand with bloating, don't we?' He then looks up for a second and waves his hand in front of a crinkled nose to demonstrate exactly what goes with bloating in case just telling me wasn't enough. At this point, the waiter draws up a chair and crosses one leg over the other and simply taps his pencil on his notepad patiently.

'Yes, that crossed my mind when I just thought what it would be like. I'm actually considering the pork in apple sauce...' I tap my finger against my chin, thinking that pork in apple sauce would be the last thing I would normally consider, but apples are healthy aren't they?

Gregory immediately puts down his menu so that I can feel the full force of his beady glare,' Pork? Really? Did you...'

I interject quickly before he ruins any possible future I might have with pork on another occasion, 'No! Not really. I was just considering that pork in apple sauce as an alternative choice in case they ran out of what I actually want which is...' I look at all the options on the menu and suddenly everything seems like it will be an issue for this man – the chicken probably came before the egg, or the lamb shank was shanked when it should have been killed humanely. I look helplessly at the waiter who shrugs at me and crosses his fingers at me again to wish me luck.

'Which is...?' Gregory prompts me. I lift my head with a confidence that I am not feeling and just go for it, 'Beef.'

The waiter squeezes my knee as if to say it's going to be okay. Well actually, it was more a brush on my mid-thigh, but I'm sure it's just that his aim is a little off.

'Beef. Yes, I think beef because I was feeling a little low on iron the other day.'

I swear I read somewhere that beef has iron in it, or was it calcium? I actually put my hand on the waiter's for support at this moment of truth and he gives me the widest grin ever – it's so nice that someone is here, willing me to make the right choice. Who'd have thought choosing a meal could be so stressful?

'Well...' Gregory starts and I hold my breath, 'grass fed beef does have the most absorbable form of iron...' he pauses, and I continue holding my breath. The waiter now has his pencil poised above his notepad in anticipation.

'...not to mention all sorts of amino acids as well as zinc to support the immune system...' he pauses thoughtfully again. He really needs to give a yay or nay because I don't think I can hold my breath for much longer. Wait...he's nodding.

'...Good choice, Gina. Especially with your iron issues.' I take a huge gasp of air in relief and both he and the waiter give me a concerned look. I smile that I'm okay and take a gulp of my drink.

'I'll have the chicken. I happen to know that beef cooked in wine sauce takes at least 30 minutes high intensity interval training to burn off in comparison to the grilled chicken. I just don't get the time.' Gregory smiles as he folds back his menu with his choice. I'm now doubly happy I chose the beef. I happen to know they over-cook it here. Even if you asked for it raw, it would arrive with chargrilled edges. I just had a thought that if his reaction isn't the right one, I can justifiably keep chewing while I compose myself to respond. As much as I'd really prefer chicken too, I don't think I'd get away with chewing indefinitely on a chicken leg. The waiter rises from the seat next to me.

'Of course, Madam. I will get that ready for you right away.' He takes my menu and kisses my hand again before turning to walk away.

'Erm...excuse me? I said I'll have the chicken, if that's okay?' Gregory holds the menu towards the waiter who looks at him hard for a few seconds, snatches the menu from his hand and walks away.

Gregory shakes his head, 'Hopefully he won't spit in my food.' I can't help laughing at that comment because the waiter looked like if he was that way inclined, he wouldn't wait for the food to do it. The conversation flows pretty much quite easily after that in the following order:

General chit chat = fifteen minutes.

Waiter back with our orders = twenty-five minutes later.

The dreaded question = thirty-two minutes and forty seconds total.

'So, might I ask you that personal question now?'

Here it comes. You can do it, Gina. Just like Lisa said. Just like you did in the toilets.

'Sure, you can ask. That doesn't mean I will answer.' You go girl, keep your cool.

'How are you available for a date with me?'

'I didn't have any appointments today, but tomorrow my schedule is...'

'No, I mean how are you still single?'

'Haven't met the right guy yet?' I laugh a little nervously

'I'm a nutritional scientist, you can't fob me off with that one. Women that look like you must meet the right guy all the time. So there has to be a really good reason why you haven't taken one up on his offer?' Gregory's beady eyes are practically boring into my soul. I'm changing my mind again. Maybe it *is* his glasses.

I smile and cut a piece of beef, shove it quickly into my mouth and chew slowly. Really slowly. I know I've rehearsed my response for hours – Lisa all but beat it into my subconscious. But with Gregory's face in front of me instead of Lisa's, my confession doesn't seem to want to roll off my tongue.

I point to my mouth and indicate that it's a really chewy piece of meat as to why I can't quite answer just yet. I'll be chewing my tongue in a minute if I don't say something soon. Come on girl, if you can (nearly) say it in the toilet, you can say it at the table.

I quickly swallow and blurt out 'I'm a virgin' and shove another piece of meat in my mouth. I'm looking at my plate now because I can't bring myself to see the look in his eyes.

All I can hear in my head is Lisa going over the plan...

'...I'm telling you, it's foolproof. I've practically been studying "Don't tell me Lies" – it's a TV program about reading people's micro expressions to know what they are thinking or if they are telling the truth. So, if he wrinkles his nose and raises his upper lip – that means he's disgusted.'

'Why would he be disgusted by what I've told him?' I gasp with concern.

'That's precisely what my question would be.' Lisa nods matter of factly even though that doesn't quite answer my question.

'Now, if hunches his shoulders, he's being evasive.'

'What would he be evasive about when I'm the one that will likely be questioned?'

'Exactly! So that would be a sure sign something is off.' Lisa wrinkles her eyes suspiciously as if she's already sizing the guy up.

'Look out for if his lip twitches and whether he averts his eyes – that's a sure sign that he's lying.'

'Okay...and how does that help me gauge how he feels about what I've said...?'

'It doesn't, but it's good to know.' Lisa waves her finger at me, 'The most important one is if he raises his eyebrows, then really opens his eyes and mouth – that means he's shocked...or is it surprised? Either way, he's probably going to be a dick about it so joke it off and switch to talking about football or Big Brother.'

'What will talking about sport or reality TV do?' I'm starting to feel apprehensive already.

'He's a man – they can't multi task or multi talk. He will totally be distracted with one or the other, so he'll barely remember that you mentioned anything about your sexual prowess – or lack thereof. Then drop your napkin so you can secretly text me and I'll shred his date sheet so you never have to see his jerk-face again.'

'What if I can't bear to sit with his jerk-face for the rest of the meal?' I'm already anticipating that will be a distinct possibility – and clearly so is my friend.

'I'll call you five minutes later to tell you there's an emergency. That'll give you the perfect excuse to dump his insensitive ass.'

A whole minute later, on hearing nothing from my date; I finally look up to see which expression I'm faced with. I've already decided that if it's not an understanding smile, then that is my cue to bring up Big Brother. I didn't need Lisa's lesson for the face I see. Gregory is grinning at me.

'Good one, Gina – seriously, what's the reason?'

He doesn't believe me. And I suddenly feel quite indignant. I mean I know my "condition" may be rare, but it's not impossible you know. I chew my beef a little quicker this time, place my fork on the plate, and look him dead in the eyes.

'I am serious.'

The expression on his face – which is not a micro one - morphs slowly from humour to shock. Yep, exactly how Lisa said. If we were in a movie, his face would be changing in slow motion. The lower his jaw drops, the wider his eyes open and the more I cringe inside as to what will come next.

'How...?' Gregory looks shell shocked right now. I'm waiting for him to finish his question, but seconds fly by and I'm still just getting the shell shocked look.

'How...did I let that happen?' I finish his obvious question. Gregory is still giving me that shocked look...oh, wait...looks like he's going to say something else now.

'What...?' Gregory starts again and then stops, still staring open mouthed at me, his beady eyes open wide, looking magnified through his glasses as he peers at me. Again, I'm waiting for something more as the seconds pass.

'What...happened?' I prompt hoping this will help. He stares at me a few more seconds before shaking his head slowly.

'When...?' And again, one word is all Gregory manages to get out as he is transfixed.

'When...did this happen? Or should I say when did this *not* happen?'

I add a little laugh at the end, hoping humour will help – and fail miserably. Gregory leans back in his seat looking totally stunned. He then leans forward in his seat, still looking stunned but also looking at me like I'm not real.

'I can't believe...I don't understand...' The strain on this man's face to try and comprehend what I've just said is making me feel a little uncomfortable now.

He tries again, 'How...?' and again, only manages to get out one word.

Okay, I knew he might be a tad shocked at hearing my sexual status, but this is something else entirely. The man's face could not be more rocked with shock. It's as if this is the most astonishing, unbelievable news he's ever heard in his life. I think I'd at least manage a "Wow!' if I heard the most astonishing, unbelievable news in my life. However, what I didn't think was I'd have to face a reaction like this. I mean, he's looking at me as if I'm something, not someone.

I can feel myself getting warm inside. It feels like everyone's eyes are on me, even though the only people looking at me are the waiter, a group of men walking through the restaurant area, a chubby man on the next table who is sloothing up spaghetti at the same time, and a guy on the table behind Gregory who quickly puts his menu in front of his face when I catch his gaze – very strange. In any case, I am feeling really weirded out right now, so time to end this. What's the plan again? Oh my gosh, what is the plan? And then I remember!

'Gotcha!' I shriek. Gregory jumps and looks at me confused

'Syke!' I shout again and point to him. And I add a laugh to top it off – another Lisa tip – then shove another piece of beef in my mouth. I can't tell yet whether the plan worked or not, he still looks a bit stunned. If he doesn't believe this was all a joke then I think I will die. On the spot. Right here, right now. I hold my breath and chew the beef at the same time – which I must say isn't as easy as it sounds.

His face slowly breaks into a smile of relief. He wags a finger at me.

'Gi-na. Gina. Gina. You really got me there!' he's still shaking his head and smiling as he tucks into his Chicken Cacciatore, which looks tastier than my leathery beef. I'm surprised I can see it through these tears that are welling up behind my lids. This was harder than I thought, but I stick with the plan anyway.

'So Gregory, do you think Arsenal should be a business first or a football team?'

Gregory cringes his nose at me, 'Can't say I'm much of a football fan.'

'Thank goodness, because what I really wanted to ask was if you watched Big Brother?'

'Of course! I wouldn't miss it for the world. Did you see last night's episode?'

And as if by magic, dinner has resumed to normality once again.

I don't know how I manage to make it to the end of dinner without choking on my beef. My napkin somehow disappeared and it would have looked really weird to suddenly drop the fork I'd been using with no trouble for the past half hour. The only other thing I could think of to drop in that moment was my phone – and you just don't drop iPhones on purpose now, do you?

I manage to just suck it up for another twenty minutes or so. He mainly talks and I just nod every few minutes so that he doesn't guess just how far away my mind really is. I then look at my watch with an exaggerated, 'Oh look at the time...!'

'Indeed, time seems to have gotten away with us. I believe I've got some marking to do also. Some of my students just can't seem to grasp that not all cholesterol is bad – your cousin being one of them

I'm afraid' Gregory tutted as he rests his napkin on the table and indicates to the waiter for the bill.

'Yes, I...erm...think she might have mentioned that.' I know she definitely mentioned that she was banking on this date going well.

'So, Gina. Any reason why we can't do this again?'

Like an automatic switch, I go into story mode.

'Well, you as an educator of fledgling minds know what it's like with busy schedules...'

'Uh huh, uh huh...' Gregory nods in concentrated agreement.

'...and I totally see how hard it must be to juggle a dating life with that kind of responsibility. Marking assignments today, guiding futures tomorrow...'

'Uh huh, uh huh...' Gregory is still nodding.

'...so it's perfectly understandable that your time is limited. So, how could I not see that, right? What kind of person would that make me if I didn't get it?' I rise from the table while Gregory is now nodding a little slower while pinching his chin.

'Thank you though. For a most educational evening.' I grab his hand and shake it with gusto. Then point my finger and thumb like a pretend gun, 'Kale and Spinach are not the same - that is simply etched on my memory now. I can see why Cousin Mona values your teachings so much.'

Gregory bows his head in a coy blush. I leave a twenty pound note on the table. Before he can protest, I put up a hand

'No, Gregory. I insist. This was more than just a dinner. It's only fair I contribute a little something, even if it can't be as enlightening as your offerings.' I salute him and then dramatically walk away. The waiter gives me a little bow as I walk past him then gives Gregory a look of disdain. He coughs impatiently at him to settle the bill, while Gregory is still scratching his head with a confused look of "what just happened?" on his face.

The crowd parts again as I walk towards the exit. They don't look like they are going to pass out, but I think I'll change my deodorant anyway – just in case.

I think Cousin Mona might do okay out of this, especially as I've made Gregory think it's him that can't commit to a second date. Guilt might just increase her grade.

I unconsciously look over to the bar area where I sat earlier. Mr Glass-sharer – who I now know to be Dave – is staring straight at me and raises his glass to me again. I don't completely ignore him this time, but instead, give a simple nod of acknowledgment as I carefully ensure I spin only once through the revolving door.

***

'So?' Lisa is breathing heavily on the other end of the phone. She'd make a good phone stalker if she ever decided to take that up.

'Well, your plan kind of worked.'

'Yes! I *knew* it must have when I didn't get the text from you!'

'But I don't think I can do that again.'

'Oh. You still felt bad?'

'Worse. I felt hopeless.'

The silence from Lisa is deafening. 'Okay, G. I'll be at yours in twenty with a bottle of your favourite Merlot, a giant bag of Skittles and an even giant-er tub of Ben and Jerry's cookie dough ice cream. I think there is more to this than even I thought. I think it's time I heard the *full* story.'

Twenty One

'So, where were we? Ah yes, the real low down as to how a chick like you managed to avoid having her car revved for all these years?'

I splutter into laughter and so does Lisa. It takes a while before we catch our breaths. I can't ever remember a time when I've been able to laugh about my situation. Lisa opens a huge carrier and pulls out a super-sized tub of Haagen Daaz. 'Mr Shah had run out of Ben and Jerry's.'

I hand her a spoon and we both get busy. We are five spoonfuls into our shared dessert and we still haven't broached the subject further than Lisa's initial introduction. I've been so long not talking about it, that now I actually want to – I just don't know where to start.

Suddenly, Lisa throws down her spoon, 'I know I should wait until you're ready to talk, but to be fair, I think the number of years I've already waited kind of gives me licence to tell you to just spill the beans already. My mind is racing right now with every spoonful with all sorts of thoughts about what could have happened for "this" not to happen. Seriously Gina, do I need to hurt somebody? Because you know I can.'

The thing is, I *do* know she can. Lisa has been learning TaeKwonDo this past year as well as already being a judo black-belter since she was ten and Nikita is her favourite program. Need I say more?

'No, you don't need to hurt anyone. Maybe at the time it might have helped. In fact, I'm sure it would have. But now, nearly 20 years down the line, I think it's a little late.'

The anger that has darkened Lisa's face shows that she would not be amiss to use her karate skills to help someone on a journey into their next life. As she starts to get to her feet in what feels like slow motion, I grab her hand to sit down again.

'No! No, it's not what you think! It's not *that*!'

The relief that replaces the anger makes me feel warm inside that I have a friend that cares so much. It also brings back that feeling of shame for not telling her sooner.

'Right. You need to just *tell* me.' Lisa folds her arms to emphasise the fact that if I don't tell her then she'll likely use her TaeKwonDo on me. I take a deep breath.

'Okay, do you remember Romeo Davis from when we were in secondary school?'

'Romeo...' Lisa is twisting her face every which way to try and think back.

'You know? The cute one that all the girls liked from Daneham Boys school?'

'Oh...Romeo the Romeo!' Lisa smiles in recognition.

'Yes, the very same.'

'What does he have to do with this? You were really quiet at school and everyone knows he liked all the flashy girls.'

'Exactly. So imagine my surprise when one day I'm walking home from school going to Aunty Joyce's house to pick up my outfit to wear to our fourth year disco...'

'Ooh yeah! Mona's Mum could whip up anything on her sewing machine back then. She made you that cool denim all-in-one you wore! And I wore a similar pink cotton one. Sigh...I loved that pink cotton all-in-one...' Lisa looks a little forlorn.

'Ahem?' I cough and snap my fingers at her to bring her back to the present. She immediately sits up straight again – fully focused on my tale.

'Sorry! I'm back. So. You saw Romeo on the way to your Aunt's. Then what happened?'

'Well, he caught up to me and we started walking and talking together.'

'About what?' Lisa leans forward.

'Just general stuff about school and if I was going to the dance...'

'Hold on...where was I that day? We always walked home together?'

'You had to leave early for a dentist appointment.'

'Oh yeah, that's when I had my dreaded braces put in. Okay, continue.'

My friend never fails to amaze me on how she can jump from one passage of time to another.

'Where was I? Oh yeah, so we were just walking and talking and he asked me if I wanted to pop to his house for a drink because he didn't live far from my Aunt's. I couldn't believe that he was even talking to me – quiet Gina. No boys were ever really interested in me at school Lisa – you were always the life and soul.'

I can see Lisa wants to say something and is making a huge effort to wait until I've finished.

'Anyway, I guess I was flattered...no, I was definitely flattered. And that took over my better judgement...because I said yes.' I close my eyes to wait for a hail of "Are you seven kinds of crazy?" to come from Lisa. But it doesn't. I open one eye slowly to see my friend looking at me with a very hard to read expression. She simply rolls her hand forward to indicate I should continue my story. As I continue, it's like I'm re-living the day all over again...

'So, where exactly do you live then? Because my aunt lives over there.' I point at number 58. I'm starting to have reservations about how good an idea this is.

'And I live right there, three doors away at number 64. I've seen you visit that house before.' Romeo smiles at me which kind of lowers my reservations. But not 100%. I think he guesses this by the way I hesitate going through the front door.

'Plus, my Mum is at home too.' I guess that was the okay I was looking for, so I follow him through.

'The kitchen is this way,' he shrugs off his jacket as he walks through. I instinctively shout out, 'Hello

Mrs Davis!' and hear a voice from the back of the house, 'Hello dear! I'm just in the middle of my daytime soaps!'

'Everything here stops between 2pm and 5pm. That's when my Mum watches her daily soaps back to back – Old Money, New Money; Barnaby Road and her all-time favourite, Mothers and Daughters.'

'My mum watches Mothers and Daughters too.'

'I don't worry though. At 5pm she'll get right back to baking so there'll still be lemon drizzle for afters. Hey, you could take your friend Lisa a slice if you want. My Mum makes the best lemon cake.' Romeo opens the fridge, 'Lemonade or orange juice?'

'She'd like that, and Orange juice is fine thanks.' I look over the kitchen. It's huge.

'I've got a TV in my room, so we can have our drinks in there.' Romeo already starts to walk out of the kitchen with the drinks before I can protest. I'll probably sound like I'm making a big deal over nothing if I do anyway. Plus, his Mum is only down the hall. I follow behind him to his room and sit on the very edge of the bed. As soon as I've walked through, he closes the door firmly behind me.

'What are you doing?' My instincts are kicking in again.

'Just making sure we have a little privacy.' He smiles innocently enough, but suddenly I'm not feeling comfortable about this.

'Why do we need privacy to drink orange juice?' I ask lightly. A lot more lightly than I'm actually feeling. He just smiles at me and walks towards me. I jump off the edge of the bed.

'I'm not that thirsty any more. Plus, my aunt is expecting me so I should go now.' Romeo looks a little surprised but doesn't move from in front of the door.

'But you just got here.' He says with a smile that shows why he always has a different girl on his arm.

'And now I've got to go.' He still doesn't move. I take a deep breath and my next words come out a lot calmer than I feel, 'and if you don't move and let me out, I am going to scream. Your mother will fly in here like a bat out of hell, and then give you hell for making her miss her soaps.'

We both stare at one another – no doubt both wondering whose bluff will be called. Will he move? Or will I scream?

With a little bow, he moves away from the door and walks around to the other side of his bed and flops across it. I smile sarcastically at him and calmly walk through. As I look back at him I shout 'I'm off now Mrs Davis.'

'See you next time, dear.' The voice from the end of the corridor shouts back. I quietly close Romeo's bedroom door behind me and can not get out of the front door quick enough, the one thought in my head being 'Oh no you will not Mrs Davis.'

When I get into the street I breathe the deepest sigh of relief. I drop a note through my aunt's letter box telling her I'll pass by another time for my outfit as something came up, and make my way home as fast as my trembling legs will carry me.

'And I vowed at that moment that I would never put myself in that situation again. I guess you could officially call that my first bad date. Now I think back, those 15 minutes directed the sexual path of the next 20 years of my life.' I smile sadly. I can feel Lisa relax as she hears my story unfold.

'Hmm...so Romeo Davis. I'm sure he still lives at his Mum's' I can see a glint in Lisa's eyes.

'Lisa, come on now. It was a really long time ago. He probably wouldn't even remember – I was one of very many. Then again, it was nearly 5pm so his Mum would have soon started baking. There wasn't Childline back then so the fear of his mother possibly taking a rolling pin to him when

I threatened to scream might have stood the test of time in his memory.'

I can just imagine Lisa karate-chopping him in the side of his neck and resting her foot in the middle of his chest as he hits the ground...I shake the image out of my head. It looks too good and like I just told Lisa, it was a long time ago.

'Okay, so how did that lead to...well, to this?' Lisa is focused on the story again.

'Well, at first I thought I was just being really careful. Guys would talk to me and as long as it was platonic it was fine, but the minute it got more personal, I would automatically find a way to put it back on a platonic plane. It's like my mind jumps straight from "Hi how you doing?" to "Baby, let's do it!"

'Is that what happened with Stu and Roger? Well, Roger doesn't really count. Anyone who wears a ponytail higher than yours should not have been in your lane in the first place. Trust me, Mr Shah did not divulge that little fact to the vetting committee.' The vetting committee, aka Lisa.

'Yeah, just like Stu and Roger but in varying degrees. I get very conscious of the fact that I'm 35 and then extremely embarrassed at the fact that I'm 35 and still a virgin and then my mind goes into auto self-preservation mode. I didn't even realise that I was doing it at first, it always seemed to be natural walking the friendship path and it wasn't that big a deal going through your teens without a boyfriend. It wasn't like I planned to not "do it".

'If you didn't plan to, how else could so many years pass by without getting that doughnut dunked?' Lisa looks sceptical and sad. She hasn't quite grasped this would not have been my conscious choice – things just turned out that way.

'You'd be surprised how fast time can fly. When I was studying, there didn't seem time for serious relationships. Then I was doing all the beauty pageants with Mum and just working all the time trying to save all my pennies so I could open my business. Before I knew it I was in my thirties, never had sex before and too embarrassed to tell anyone about it. And as I get a little older it gets worse. Acute and ground-swallowing-ly worse. Unless you've experienced it, you just couldn't comprehend how it feels to be a sexual infant in an adult's body at such a late period in your life.'

'Have you never thought of just going with someone who you actually think you would like to do it with? You would have no shortage of offers

Gina and the fact that it would be with someone that you already know and liked might not make you feel so anxious.'

'I did consider that once. With someone I didn't know in case things didn't go accordingly. I did actually try once. To, you know.'

'And what happened?'

'It wouldn't go in.'

'What do you mean?'

'I mean just that. "It" wouldn't go "in".'

'And you've blamed yourself for all these years because some bozo couldn't get it up?'

'That's the thing. The bozo *did* get it up. Nancy wouldn't let him in.'

'Huh? Who's Nancy? And what does she have to do with all this?'

'Nancy...' I point towards my private lady parts.

'Oh...*that's* Nancy.' Lisa smiles.

'She just shut up shop when he tried to get in.'

'Ooh...' Lisa contorts her face in sympathy.

'It was like she had a mind of her own and she would not release those gates no matter what he tried. In the end we just had to call it a day. He looked at me so strangely but apologised saying it was his fault. But I knew he knew it wasn't really his fault. I just went along with it and could not leave soon enough. I was both too acutely embarrassed to contradict him and ecstatically happy that I would never have to see him again.'

'Ooh...' Lisa covers her eyes.

'Yeah. I'll never forget that look. So the option of trying again with someone that I *did* know was never going to happen after that. It was not an experience I wanted to repeat with anyone.'

Lisa starts to protest but I put my hand up to stop her.

'I would feel even *more* anxious with someone I knew. I wouldn't be able to fake that I was experienced. I'd have to tell them. And what if they didn't understand? What if I really liked them and they didn't understand? Just act like I'm a freak or something? After what happened with the person I didn't know, the risk of the same thing happening with someone I did know just seemed too great. And much too embarrassing to contemplate again.'

'And no-one has ever suspected that this could be the reason why you're on your own? After all this time?' Lisa now looks amazed.

'Did you?' I ask cocking my head to the side. She acknowledges by looking down at the ground.

'What happens instead is that I just get judged. Everyone thinking that I think I'm too nice to go out with regular guys. Or that I'm too picky or too fussy or probably even a lesbian.'

'No, they don't think you're a lesbian. Well, at first they did, until Trina from the end of the road who "came out" last year said she'd know if you were – even though we didn't know that she was. I think lesbians maybe have a radar or something? Anyway, everybody still just thinks you're too picky.' Lisa says matter-of-factly to my look of shock, 'What? It's not like you don't already know that people talk. I mean, have you looked in the mirror lately? You are gorgeous – even to the Trina's of the world.' Lisa gets up and starts pacing.

'I still say though, if you haven't actually told anyone – apart from me,' Lisa looks proud as she says that, 'then you don't really know for sure that they'll think it's as bad as you think they'll think it is.'

'I have told someone, so I do know for sure. I told Gregory remember? Cousin Mona's teacher? He was the one we decided to try your plan out on first.'

'Gina, it was a sound plan!' Lisa protests

'In theory it was. In practise, not so much. I did everything just like you said and his reaction was exactly like I imagined. His shocked expression made me feel like an alien. I knew he automatically thought there was something wrong with me. And why wouldn't he? I think there must be something wrong with me too.'

'But you brushed it off by following the plan!'

'In front of him maybe, but not to myself! If I felt like an alien before – which I did - then I surely feel even worse now after that little episode. And I didn't ever think *that* would be possible.'

'Surely, it can't be that bad...' Lisa looks at me and then lowers her eyes. Even she can't think of any more words of encouragement. The only positive out of this is that I'm not going through it on my own anymore.

'It can and it is, Lisa. Can you possibly even imagine for a minute how it must feel to *be* 35 years old and never had sex? When every other program on television shows people half your age doing it like rabbits? And on top of that, I saw your neighbour Tilly the other day and she is already thinking about putting her fourteen-year-old daughter Angel on contraception. Seriously, I feel like a freak of nature.'

Lisa crosses her arms and curls her lip, 'Hmph. Angel is the one that's a little freak, not you. From twelve, she was already in high heels, mini skirts and climbing out of her bedroom window in the dead of night. I even saw her at the health clinic the other day picking up free condoms. But if you ask me, that was already on the cards for the kid with a name like that.'

'So, possibly sexually active at twelve, not four-teen. My mistake. Now, doesn't that just change everything.' I'm not even trying to keep the sar-casm out of my voice, 'I've been on Earth nearly three times as long as that and barely managed to make it to foreplay. Yeah, that makes me feel SO much better.'

I feel so frustrated and hopeless right now, it takes a mighty effort to hold the tears back.

'Gina, you *do* know that it's nothing to be ashamed of, right?' Lisa reaches for my arms. I can feel the concern emanating from her very being.

'That is so easy for you to say but it's not the 1940's anymore where it's the done thing to hold onto your virtue until someone proposes to you. When something that is meant to be so special just feels like something to be rid of ASAP. Just so you can feel normal instead of abnormal because you haven't managed to take a test drive when so many other females half your age have already driven the car in every direction *and* parked it up! The cold hard fact of the matter is that I should be the Master by now, not still the young grasshopper.'

'Oh phooey. Driving is overrated anyway. And Chinese movies too! Besides, maybe that's what we need. To bring back some of those old fashioned values.'

'Really? For goodness sakes they sell soap powder with sex! Trust me; those values you speak of are not coming back any time soon. Let's face it, Old Virginia now isn't just about whisky, it's about me. I'm on track to be the first pensioner virgin. If you put me in a cage, you could sell tickets - I'm definitely one of a kind.'

'Gina stop! You are not going to be a pensioner virgin! Look, we are living in the twenty-first century. There must be virgins your age everywhere.' I give her a look.

'Like where? In fact, name me one. Name me just one thirty-something virgin you know whose name is not Gina?'

I can literally see the muscles flexing in Lisa's mind. It's a lot of mental effort for nothing, if you ask me because I already know she doesn't know anyone out there like me. *I* don't even know anyone out there like me despite me telling Candy and Tina in the toilets otherwise.

'Well, I can't pinpoint a particular person or area they might congregate, but I am confident they are out there. Almost.' Lisa has the good grace to look sheepish

'See? Almost!' Before I can go into one again Lisa grabs a hold of my hand.

'Okay, okay, I don't know any other virgins and you are in fact the first one I've met BUT that's full stop, not because you're over 30. I've just never met a virgin before at any age.

I raise an eyebrow and look at her.

'Gina, people are going to react no matter what – but it's not because of your age, it's because you're the hottest bachelorette in town. Okay, maybe it's a little because of your age but definitely mainly because you are the hottest bachelorette in town. Anyone would expect that someone who looks like you would have had her hymen broken by a never ending queue of guys, so it's a given there's gonna be surprise to hear your dong hasn't been dinged.'

'Lisa, as I said before – who feels it knows it. You can't really appreciate how I feel because you got your...your dong dinged at a normal age – which 35 isn't no matter how much you try to put a spin on it. It's a strange phenomenon and it's not like there's a support group or a help-me-I'm-a-virgin .com website where I can go and discuss all-things virgin like or my non-existent sexperience.'

'Well, there is now – I'm your support group. I said we would fix this and we will. We will get a key in that lock if it kills me and we will find the right person to turn that key by sticking to the plan.' Lisa finishes with determination.

'Lisa, there's...'

'Before you say there's no point, there is! Right now your heart is linked to your hooch so we have to sort one in order to release the other. That is the point, and it's a point worth fighting for. Don't you want a boyfriend, Gina? To talk to on the phone until 2.30am in the morning? To RSVP on an invitation that you and your partner will be pleased to attend rather than you and me?' Lisa is holding onto both my hands and staring into my eyes earnestly. I give a big sigh.

'Of course I want those things, who doesn't want those things! But...'

'No buts then! Because there's no way I'm go-ing to allow my best friend to miss out on kissing, cuddling, hand holding and multiple orgasms with a proper boyfriend. That's just not going to happen on my watch. We just need to practice the plan a bit more, work on your delivery...' Lisa tapers off and starts rubbing her chin and pacing. It's clear she's already thinking about how to fix this. There's no reasoning with her when she gets a plan in her head. But this is no ordinary situation to plan for. As much as I would trust my best friend with my life, trusting her with this is a whole lot trickier because if it goes wrong, then the life I'd trust her with won't be worth living.

Twenty Two

'Okay everyone, settle down now. It's not a party, we're here to find Gina a date.' Lisa takes a bite of Mum's freshly baked apple pie and delicately brushes some crumbs away from her face.

'Now, I think we could do with a real catch this time. Someone particularly charming, who must also be understanding. No judgy people...oh and sensitive. Yeah, sensitivity is a definite must...' Lisa mumbles this last bit almost to herself and starts scribbling on her clipboard.

'Why all this sudden additional criteria? Aren't we just supposed to be giving her the helping hand she so desperately needs? A date is a date isn't it?' Delilah looks up from one of my magazines that Dad was flicking through at the last meeting (that I still haven't managed to read yet) delaying her spoonful of apple pie from disappearing down her cheeky gob. One of her eyebrows is raised suspiciously at the same time as mine is raised with concern. And not just at the fact she said I'm desperate. We both look over to Lisa who is calmly staring my nemesis in the eye.

'Delilah, wouldn't we be doing our friend a disservice if we didn't at least try to attempt to find her someone as tender and understanding as your Paul?'

Delilah stares at Lisa hard for a few more seconds before dismissing the matter with a wave of her hand and another spoonful of pie. I don't fail to notice the smug smile on her face – courtesy of Lisa suggesting that Delilah's guy is in a class of his own. I suppose it wouldn't have done my cause much good to add soppy and whipped to that list.

Mum cuts a large slice of apple pie and hands it to Mr Shah.

'Hmph, my Stu was *particularly* sensitive. Some people just don't know a good man when their Mother sees one.' Mum slides me a sideways look. Okay, I guess it's now confirmed that she hasn't quite forgiven me yet for not bearing Stu's children.

'What about you Mr Robbins? Don't you know anyone who could treat your daughter how you treat your lovely Mrs Robbins?' Lisa directs the conversation to my Dad. Mum beams with pride like a morning star and smacks Cousin Mona's hand as she reaches for a slice of pie and instead takes it straight over to Lisa.

'Have another slice dear. And if you wait one moment, I'll bring you some of my home made custard to go with it. I know you're partial to a bit of custard with your apple pie rather than cream.'

'Why, thank you Mrs Robbins!' Lisa pokes her tongue out at Cousin Mona who shakes her head and starts tapping on her phone again.

'Well, Mr Robbins? Any ideas?' Lisa prompts my Dad again.

'I'm just here for the cake, love.' My Dad looks over to me and gives me a wink. Ever my ally, I couldn't love him more right now

Gran is gently fanning herself like a Pharaoh's wife.

'Well, if anyone cares to ask. I think I have the perfect candidate.' Gran is a renowned master matchmaker – if she says he's perfect, he probably is. Dammit.

'Of course. We're all ears Grandma Robbins. Hit it.' I think if she had the opportunity, Lisa could really take this role she's playing to a professional level.

'He's the son of one of my Bridge partners at the Over 60 Shades of Grey Seniors Club.'

'Ooh, I've always wanted to play Bridge.' Mum's eyes light up as she arrives back with the custard for Lisa's pie.

'Me too!' chimes Paula, who I'm clearly giving too much free time to if she can now make these meetings. 'My great Aunt Nessie – she was named after the Loch Ness Monster – was teaching me last year when she came to visit.'

I so want to ask why her great Aunt's parents felt it was appropriate to name their daughter after a monster, but I'll save that one for another day.

'You're all more than welcome to come to the Club. We have a Newbies Night on Thursdays for Under Agers and this week...'

'Ahem!' Lisa coughs loudly to get everyone's attention, 'as you were saying Grandma Robbins... about your bridge partner's son?'

'Ah yes, Tomlinson. Everyone calls him Tom except me. The way I see it, if his mother took the time to get Tomlinson printed on his birth certificate then it doesn't seem right to just cut his name in half. Anyway, he brings his grandmother Eileen to the Club every other Thursday and then every other *other* Thursday he stays and plays a few rounds with us. Now, you can't get more sensitive than that.' Gran flicks her fan in Lisa's direction and gives me a wink, 'Not to mention that he is utterly drop-dead handsome and is an heir to the family business of Launderettes.'

Delilah sniggers, 'A launderette Heir? There's really such a thing?'

'There is and his inheritance is not to be sneezed at. His family own the second largest number of launderettes in the country, and at last count, that was 486. Did you know that a launderette on a busy council estate could average gross takings of over £70,000 annually? Times that by 486! Do the math honey; it's not rocket science to figure out that even after expenses that leaves a tidy profit.'

Delilah's eyes open wide as she does the math in her head while gobbling another rather large spoonful of pie and comes up with what must be a juicy figure.

'Ooh, maybe he could give us a deal on a new washing machine. Our one has been on the blink ever since your father was trying to be helpful and washed his pants with the belt still in and his pocket full of change. It's just never quite been the same since.' Mum sighs as she cuts a piece of pie and finally hands it to Cousin Mona.

'What, no custard for me Aunty? You know your homemade custard is my favourite.' Cousin Mona flutters her eyes at Mum.

'Of course dear. I'll just fetch you some. Won't be a moment. It should still be nice and warm on my new food warmer, should only need a quick stir.' Mum pats her niece on the shoulder and hustles back to the kitchen. Cousin Mona smugly pokes her tongue back out at Lisa.

'I don't think he actually sells washing machines Mrs Robbins,' Lisa shouts so that Mum can hear her from the kitchen, 'but good thinking as he's bound to know a man who does. Actually, I might ask him about one for my mum too...' Lisa starts scribbling again on her clipboard.

'Anyway, I happen to know he is single and it's his week to play bridge with us,' Gran resumes her fanning, 'I'm sure he wouldn't mind cutting his game short for a date with my gorgeous grand-daughter. I know the doorman wouldn't mind either, but I would – he's far too close to your late grandfather's age.' Gran winks at me and then waves my new royal blue appointment diary at Lisa, 'And according to Virginia's diary, she's free too.'

I really need to find a way to steal that appointment diary back. But then again, if she made a copy before...

'That's perfect Grandma Robbins, can I leave you to organise that?' Lisa does not even raise her head from her essay on the clipboard. Gran points to the smart phone at her ear, 'Already on it...Ahh, yes Eileen my dear, I'm calling about your grandson Tomlinson...' Gran's voice tails off as she leaves the room to continue sorting out my love life.

'Ahem,' Delilah coughs to get everyone's attention, 'I believe I may have a candidate to offer also. His name is Oliver but he's on vacation at the moment so I'd rather wait to confirm with him before making it official.'

'I tell you what Delilah, we'll put a provisional date booking in for him. Grandma Robbins should be sorting out next Thursday, so how about we pencil in the Thursday following that – give your pal some time to get back from holiday and re-acclimatise. I'm happy to slot it in now, that's how confident I am your guy will confirm it'll be okay. Take note Gina. Two weeks today – 7.30pm Rymans – date with Delilah's candidate. Delilah, tell him to wear a white carnation.' Lisa gives Delilah a wink who gives her a dirty look in response. The thought that someone might want to date me without even an introduction clearly irks her. And anything that irks Delilah gives me a warm glow inside. I won't even think about who she would want to set me up with – she probably won't do her worst even though she'd love to purely because she believes if I'm off the market then it will erase my pre-teen two-week date with her other half, out of her mind.

Everything seems a little surreal since my full blown revelation to Lisa yesterday. I've never spoken about it to anyone before and I guess it's still sinking in that I finally have. In fact, I haven't even really thought about the situation I got into back then – just lived with the consequences. I feel surprisingly vulnerable right now. Like I've handed over access to information that could ruin my life or something.

My eyes meet Lisa's for a few seconds and she nods her understanding at me and winks that everything is going to be okay. I welcome the confirmation that I couldn't have chosen a better person to share this burden with. I look across the room at everyone. Delilah and Patsy are eating pie and talking about what lingerie would knock

Paul's socks off for their fifth anniversary. Dad is flicking through another of my magazines - I think he's doing one of those dating quizzes! Cousin Mona, as expected, is flicking through her phone whilst Mr Shah is watching TV and bobbing his head to some Bollywood musical. All of these people are here to help me find someone and eat Mum's baking. None of them are thinking for a moment, that it could actually be my choice to stay single because of a big secret. I suddenly feel a frisson of guilt, but this soon passes when I think if none of this had happened, I may never have gotten to this point where the thought of having sex one day might actually be possible for me.

Gran is back with a satisfied smile, 'It's all arranged. Eileen said she'll make sure Tomlinson sticks around next Thursday after the bridge game. She's quite looking forward to the possibility of our grandchildren getting together.' Gran chuckles and resumes her fanning again. Lisa grabs her smart phone, 'Let me call Rymans right now while it's fresh in my mind...'

'Please, no! Not Rymans again. Can I have a date somewhere else for a change?' Funnily enough, the first thing that really comes to mind is not that people might start to think Rymans is my local pick up bar – which technically it sort of is – but that I didn't want to bump into Dave again with yet another date. Lisa pauses, clearly racking her brains to think of another date place. Since when did Rymans become the only gig in town?

'The Club has a rather charming bar with a real log fire. In fact, it's quite romantic...' Gran's eyes are suddenly glinting at the notion.

'Ooh, a real log fire,' Mum is in reminisce mode, 'Hey Henry, do you remember when we stayed at that lodge and there was that fire in the waiting room?'

Dad taps his pencil on his nose to jog his memory, 'If I remember rightly, that was a flame cake that went wrong. The waiter brought it in and started to sing happy birthday when one of the guests started to choke. He put the cake on the table so he could give her the Heimlich Manoeuvre and everyone was so engrossed that they forgot about the cake?'

'Hmm...I vaguely remember...'

'Only vaguely Joan? Seriously? The manager had to put the fire out with a mini fire extinguisher, then asked everyone whether they wanted a well done slice with custard or ice cream.'

'Ah yes! That's right dear. How could I not remember? The sponge was so light – even if a little charred around the edges.'

'That's a done deal then – 8.00pm at the Over 60 Shades of Grey Seniors Club bar with real log fire it is then. That's a wrap folks, see you all next week.' Lisa finishes her note with a flourish but no one seems to be making a move to leave.

I cough to get everyone's attention and clap my hands, 'Lisa said it's a wrap? Meeting adjourned? Gathering over?'

Everyone looks at me in surprise before starting to make a beeline towards the front door. Everyone except Delilah, who just looks inconvenienced and is rushing to finish her pie.

As everyone files out of the house, Lisa – who is the last to leave – puts her hand on my shoulder and stares deeply into my eyes.

'Stick to the plan. Practice makes perfect. Wisdom is as wisdom does.'

If she's waiting for a reaction, she'll have to wait until I can figure out what wisdom is as wisdom does means. If I was wise, I'd have shagged the first guy that came along years ago – just spread my legs and thought of England. Then again, Nancy would no doubt have put a stop to that. Still, it's going to be different this time. I *do* actually want this date for all the reasons Lisa so eloquently enumerated. And how bad can it go anyway? He's a Launderette Heir for goodness sakes. How many of them do you come across every day? Plus, his reaction can hardly be worse than the last guy's can it?

Twenty Three

As I get closer to the Over 60 Shades of Grey Seniors Club where my Gran hangs out, I start to think of my date ahead. It feels a bit weird that this time the plan is now *not* to figure out a story to prevent a second date.

The elderly doorman is kind of slouching against the door. He immediately seems to perk as I approach the club entrance. An older man – not that much older than the doorman at a guess - with a walking stick gets to the door just before me, then abruptly starts walking backwards. The doorman is standing behind him whispering something into his ear. As I get to the door, the doorman tips his hat to me and gives me a big grin and a four tooth smile.

'Evening Gorgeous. Ladies first.' The doorman looks pointedly at the elderly gentleman as he says this, who looks just as hard back at him, tapping his stick on the ground still trying to move forward.

I'm so glad Gran has age-appropriate boundaries and did not think it suitable to add this doorman to Lisa's dating list. Mum, on the other hand, would not have been so selective. Trying to persuade Lisa to add Bill the postman - who is retiring next year and Ben the school keeper who is retiring *this* year, is kind of telling.

'Hello.' I nod politely and smile at both of them as I push through the door. The backward walking man barely acknowledges me as he still struggles to move forward, glaring at the doorman who also seems to be putting a lot of effort into...it appears, just standing there.

As I walk into the lobby, something makes me turn to look back at the two men. If I wasn't so sure I must be mistaken, I would swear I saw the elderly doorman holding onto the even more elderly man's trouser belt, but why would he do that? Hence, why I must be imagining things. I shrug and continue to the designated meeting spot.

The bar in this place really is nice – just like Gran said. The log fire looks genuine enough, doesn't resemble a flambé dessert at all. I make my way towards the armchair closest to the fire. I look at my watch and see it's just after 8pm. Tomlinson's bridge game must have run over. The dancing flames are having a kind of hypnotic effect on me and seconds later I am kicking off my shoes. As my eyes start to waver, I'm tapped on the shoulder. I sleepily look up expecting to meet the eyes of Tomlinson, but the sight makes me bolt upright and start scrambling for my shoes.

'You look very peaceful when you are sleeping.' Dave is perched on the arm rest of my chair

'Seriously, are you stalking me?' I self-consciously start to smooth my must-be-ruffled hair.

'I could say the same thing. I've been bringing my Grandfather here to play chess every Tuesday and I've never seen *you* here before.'

'Erm, in case you didn't realise – it's Thursday today.'

'Yeah, they changed the day this week to Thursday. Mr Bergemire – my Grandfather's chess partner had a hospital appointment on Tuesday for an ingrowing toenail.'

'Oh...I see.'

'So, what are you doing here?'

'I'm meeting a ...a friend.' I smooth down my skirt defensively. I don't even know why I'm feeling defensive. So what if every time he's seen me, I'm meeting some guy? – It's not like that's a crime.

'I see. Your taste in friends appears to have...matured if you're now meeting them in the Over 60 Shades of Grey Seniors Club. Didn't the name give you a hint?' Dave can barely hide the smirk on his face.

'What? No...No! Ugh, please!' I cringe my distaste at his unspoken suggestion. He holds up his hands in laughter.

'Not that I owe you an explanation, but I'm meeting my Gran's friend's son if you must know. He brings his Gran Eileen here to play bridge every other Thursday and then joins the game every other *other* Thursday. Which just so happens to be today.' I flick my hair indignantly.

'So, you're meeting another...friend then. You really are on a mission aren't you? To make a new...friend?' Dave cocks his head to the side in genuine interest.

'More like my best friend and family are on a mission. They feel I need a new... friend more than I do.' I answer in monotone without even thinking. Dave squints his eyes at me and I can already guess that he wants to ask me something else but as me and Lisa didn't practice what my response would be for questions from non-dates, I'm not going to give him a chance to ask. I make a big show of looking at my watch and see it's 8.20pm. Where *is* this Tomlinson guy anyhow?

'I happen to know that today is also the day of the bridge marathon – and the marathons can get a little crazy. It's probably overrun,' Dave bends towards me and starts speaking out the side of his mouth as if he's telling me something he shouldn't.

'I also happen to know that Mr Canning accused Mrs Denby of cheating because she won three games in a row. She hit him on the head with her handbag which made his hearing aid malfunction so the medics are trying to fix it.' Dave folds his arms matter-of-factly. It's on the tip of my tongue to ask how he knows so much about the goings on in the Seniors Club but then he'll tell me something that will endear him to me like he volunteers to read to the seniors once a week or something and then that might open a can of worms that even the early bird won't be able to catch. So I don't.

'Thanks for the detailed explanation. I guess I'd better go see if my date is involved in any of the craziness.'

I reach for my purse and walk towards the door. Now, which way is the bridge room?

'To your left, second door on your right.'

I look back at Dave who seems to have developed this uncanny knack of reading my mind, and he salutes me with that cheeky grin of his. I nod my thanks and move towards the directions I've been given.

As I reach the door, I can hear raspy loud voices and a well-spoken voice trying to calm the raspy voices down. I push open the door and my jaw drops at the sight. Gran is standing on a table shouting and pointing towards a man holding his hearing aid in one hand and waving a walking stick in the other, at two uniformed people who are trying to approach him.

One elderly lady is waving her handbag at another similarly aged woman who is using an oversized cushion as a shield. Trying to keep them apart is the well-spoken voice I heard outside the door, who also happens to be super tall and dressed in a striped blazer and super tight jeans.

The well-spoken man turns to me and says, 'Grab her, quickly! GRAB HER!'

I look around in confusion as he viciously nods his chin towards the woman with the bag. Now, Bag lady looks like she can handle herself, so I tentatively approach her in the hope that a physical intervention will not be necessary.

'Erm...hello? Excuse me, can you put down the bag and step away from it.' I speak in an authoritative tone I learnt from watching police shows on TV. Surprisingly, Bag lady stops waving her bag at Oversize- Cushion woman and stares at me. In fact, everyone goes silent and stares at me. I'm feeling quite chuffed that with just a few firm words, I've managed to calm this volatile situation down. Suddenly Bag lady lets out a war cry and comes charging towards me, bag high in the air!

The man fending off the uniformed staff – who I believe might just be Mr Canning who Dave mentioned earlier - suddenly turns towards me with a toothless grin and a leery wink.

'I'll thave you thweet thing!' he cries with a lisp and barges one of the uniformed staff out of the way then starts hobbling in the direction of Bag Lady with determination, waving his walking stick at her like a sword fighting Musketeer.

Before I can react myself and flee as fast as my heels can carry me – which wouldn't have been far because I forgot to clasp them back properly in the bar - Gran sails off the table like a Geriatric Supergirl and grapples Bag lady to the ground, 'Don't you dare! That's my granddaughter!'

The flying tackle winds Bag lady long enough for some more uniformed people to burst through the doors like Storm troopers, grab the weaponised handbag and eventually subdue her. The two uniformed staff at the same time manage to finally extricate Mr Canning from his walking stick while he shouts 'What's that you're thaying? I'm trying to thave that lovely lady!'

Striped jacket man is comforting Cushion woman with his arm around her shoulder's, 'There, there Grandmother Eileen, They've got Mrs Denby now. It's all over.'

'I only said to her that it wasn't nice to attack people if they comment on your winning streak, and she went for me!' Grandmother Eileen is still shaking as her grandson helps her walk towards a chair.

'I saw it all Grandmother. Totally unprovoked attack.' He turns to me with a toothy smile, 'Thank you so much for helping out there. Sometimes the bridge games can get rather testy, especially when character aspersions are cast.' He holds out his hand to shake mine, but before he can introduce himself, my very own Super Gran gets in there first.

'Ah Virginia, I see you've met Tomlinson. Tomlinson, this is my granddaughter Virginia.'

'Hello Virginia.'

'Please, call me Gina.'

'Not the most standard start to our introduction to say the least.' Tomlinson helps his grandmother settle into a seat and Gran sits beside her.

'Off you two go and get acquainted. I'll stay with Eileen. It's about time for a cuppa anyway.'

Tomlinson kisses his grandmother on the forehead, who still looks a bit shaken by the whole experience but pats his hand to indicate she's okay. He then offers me his arm and leads me back to the bar room with the log fire. I look around quickly to see if Dave is still lurking but thankfully he's not around.

'May I get you a drink?' Tomlinson gives me a little bow. If I didn't know his fortune was from launderettes, I'd think he was a Viscount or something. He's so proper. I think I'm a little in awe right now, but hopefully I'm managing to keep that in check.

'A peach schnapps please.' Not because it's my favourite, but like a wine spritzer, it just sounds like a classy drink. While Tomlinson gets the drinks in, I gaze into the flickering flames contemplating how this date will be different from the last. The fire is having that effect on me again and it's all I can do to keep my shoes on.

Luckily, Tomlinson isn't gone long and he's soon back with my peach schnapps and what looks like a gin and tonic for himself. He settles into the chair opposite me.

'So Tomlinson...'

'Please, call me Tom. Tomlinson is rather a mouthful and rather reminds me of my Grandmother's pet cat.' He sort of guffaws a laugh and I politely smile in response.

'So Tom,' I start again, 'You come and play regularly with your Grandmother Eileen and her friends? That's commendable.'

'Yes, I love bridge and I love my Grandmother so what better way to enjoy two of my favourite things, right? Haw, haw!' he guffaws again then takes a delicate sip of his gin and tonic.

'I guess.' Is all I can think to say in response.

'Besides, you can really learn a lot from that generation. They have a lot of interesting stories to tell. It's always a blast.'

I smile in agreement; I can sit down for hours talking to Gran when she starts going on about the Better Days.

'Tell me about it. Has your Gran Eileen told you the one about when in her day...'

And that was the way the conversation progressed for the next hour. Both of us sharing stories about our grandparents. It's been so refreshing speaking to someone who has such a healthy respect for Senior Citizens. I wonder if he has Spanish roots?

'I'm thinking some nibbles would be fab. Are you peckish? They do a rather splendid menu of starters here, would you like to partake?' Tom speaks so ye-olde-worldly. I kind of like it.

'Yes please, kind sir. That would be quite lovely.' I put on my finest posh accent to which he responds by giving me a strange look.

'Righty-o then, I'll just order a selection. Be back in a tick.' Tom throws over his shoulder as he strides over to the serving corner. I'm quite conscious that it's getting to about that time when the more personal questions start to fly. I suddenly decide to ask that question before I have to answer it for a change.

Tom is soon back with an assortment of snacks which look very appetising. We both nibble on a few in companionable but hungry silence. Surprisingly, the silence isn't awkward considering we've only just met. I decide this is the perfect opportunity to pop the question.

'So Tom, how comes your single? I would have thought an heir to a Laundromat fortune would have been swooped up by now.'

'Indeed, it is for just that reason why I have found it rather complex to find a suitable mate. They seem fine until they hear that I'm an heir...haw haw. I do believe I just cracked a joke – hear I'm an heir? Haw haw.' Tom slaps his thigh. I smile and nod politely. In truth, I didn't find it quite as funny as he did.

'Sorry, where was I? Ah yes, once they hear my business is launderettes their eyes glaze over at first – after all one wouldn't automatically think of launderettes as a money spinner I guess. But then I get a call usually by the next day and their interest in me has suddenly peaked. That's when I know they've had a chance to Google me and how much a single Laundromat can make.' He sighs as if it's

the most terrible thing in the world to have someone want you for your money. I'd happily swap my
problem with his.

'Poor...you?' I say, more as a question than a
statement.

'I don't get that impression from you though.
Your Grandmother told my Grandmother that
you have your own business?'

'Yes, selling women's underwear.'

'I find independent women are less likely to be
into me because of my money.'

'Oh...kay.' He's deduced I'm not a gold digger.
That's a compliment. I think.

'So, Gina. May I ask why you're still aloft on
the shelf?' Tom leans forward, as if he doesn't
want to miss what I'm going to say. Suddenly I
don't know if I can be bothered to go through that
whole pre-prepared response malarkey tonight. I
feel quite drained after narrowly escaping being
clobbered with a Yves Saint Laurent handbag. I'm
just going to tell him. Reaction be damned.

'I'm a virgin.' I blurt quite bluntly without
thinking. Tom nods slowly in understanding.

'Right, right. So, too busy with the business to
concentrate on men.'

I look at him as if he didn't hear me.

'No, I'm still single because I'm a virgin.' I say again.

'I see...Family commitments can be demanding. This has been my personal experience also.' Tom takes another sip of his gin and tonic. I lean forward and wave my fingers in front of his face to see if he can see me as he seems to be responding to someone else's answers.

'Did you hear what I said Tom?' I squint my eyes at him

'Of course, I have 20/20 hearing.'

'So you heard me say that I'm a virgin?'

'Yes, yes I did.' Tom nods vigorously with a wide smile.

'You understand that I'm telling you the reason I'm single is because I have never done it with a guy before.' I never thought I'd be trying to persuade someone to hear my long-kept secret.

'I do indeed understand. Completely. The first time meeting someone new can be rather daunting, to say the least.' Tom pats my hand.

'Daunting - like not ever having had sex.'

'Also having to look at the world through the eyes of another person can feel a little odd sometimes.'

'Odd - for having waited so long to have sex.'

'But overall having a relationship can be a positive experience.'

'Even for someone who has no experience. In sex.'

'Can I get you another drink?' Tom chucks back the last of the G&T in his glass.

'Sure, can I have a *Virgin* Mary please?'

'Of course, back in a tick.'

Did that really happen? I have just told this guy in as many ways as I can that I'm a virgin and he appears to be selectively ignoring the virgin parts. I'd feel like tearing my hair out if I hadn't just paid over £100 for this new keratin treatment. I can't believe I am trying to persuade this guy to believe what I am telling him. Lisa was right. It certainly got easier to say I was a virgin. I've never said it so many times in one conversation. I'm thrown. Me and Lisa didn't practice this scenario so I'm not quite sure what to do now. Tom is soon back with my cocktail and a bottle of beer for himself. I'm too fascinated about what just passed to leave the topic alone.

'So, you get what I've been telling you, right?'

'I get that people say many things for many reasons.'

'And what could the reason be to say that they were a virgin if they weren't?'

'I find that an impossible notion to contemplate, therefore I'm not even going to try.'

'So even if the reason is true, if it's not what you can contemplate, then you...just disregard it?' I'm so incredulous at this line of thinking that I can't even keep it out of my voice. He smiles at me knowingly.

'Look at you Gina. I'm sure I'm not the first to tell you that you're an extremely attractive woman.'

'So, an attractive woman, can't be a virgin?'

'An attractive woman...*your* age...?' Tom tails off, leans back in his chair and smiles before taking a swig of his beer.

'So, you really think I'm making all this up?'

'I think that is quite a distinct possibility.'

'But why would I make up that I'm a virgin of all things?'

'You have your reasons.'

'And what could they be?'

'That would be known only by you I would imagine.'

'Okay, ask me what the reason could be.'

'I'd rather not pry.'

'Please pry.'

'It's not my place to insist on information that is not freely offered.'

'I *have* freely offered it!'

'That may be so.'

'...So?'

'So?'

'So why would I make up that I am a virgin?'

'You have your reasons.'

We go around in this same circle a few more times until I feel like I want to scream. In fact, I think I will. Aaagh! I really didn't expect our conversation to be me defending the right of older women to be virgins, but I have to admit, it's been an interesting debate so far.

And no matter what I say and how I say it, he won't believe I've never had sex before... it's actually quite incredible!

'So what's the actual reason you've chosen Singledom, Gina?'

'You were right the first time Tom, just busy I guess.' Why flog a dead horse, right?

'Well Gina, I've had a pleasant evening. I hope we can do it again sometime. I know you're a busy business owner, so I will leave our future contact in your hands, shall I?'

'It was interesting meeting you too. It's getting a little late now so you might want to check on your Grandmother?' I evade his question.

'Goodness yes! Better check to see that the Old Dear isn't traumatised.' He jumps out of his seat.

'Tell my Gran, I'll see her tomorrow too.'

'Of course, of course!' He quickly pecks me on the cheek, then rushes off to tend to his relative. I can't wait to speak to Lisa. She will never believe this.

* * *

'Lisa. He didn't believe me.'

'That you didn't want to date him again?'

'No. That I was a virgin.'

'What do you mean?'

'I mean just that.'

'Just what?'

'That he didn't believe me.'

'About what?'

'That I was a virgin.'

'What do you mean?'

'I mean just that.'

'Just what?'

'THAT HE DIDN'T BELIEVE THAT I WAS A VIRGIN!'

Aaaagh!

Twenty Four

I am so glad to just have a normal day at work after some of these crazy dates. Tomlinson Jones. He is top of my list of cray cray. I so love some of these Americanisms – they can be SO much more appropriate than anything English slang has to offer – apart from maybe loopy. That admittedly is up there with cray cray. And Tomlinson is definitely both.

I mean who listens to a whole conversation but totally dismisses the part when a 35-year-old tells them they are a virgin? A loopy cray cray person that's who. There can be no other explanation.

Well, this is the first time I have had something to smile about when it comes to my sexless situation. The sun is shining, I'm out to lunch and I think it's just going to be a great day.

'Oomph!'

Until the wind is knocked out of me.

'Delilah? Is that you?' I look at the person in a crumpled heap on the floor surrounded by bags. Of all the people in all the world to bump into, it has to be Delilah. I clearly spoke too soon about it being a good day.

'I am *so* sorry! I didn't see you!'

'That would only be because you weren't looking where you were going.' Delilah somewhat ungracefully clambers back to an uptight position and smooths down her hair.

'Let me help you pick up your...'

'NO! I mean, no. Thank you. It's okay, I've got it.' She quickly grabs up her fallen bags and actually smiles at me. In fact, could she beam any harder? She's never this smiley when she sees me, especially since I nearly knocked her into next week.

'Okay then. Just offering to help.'

'Well, I'm fine. Luckily for you, no damage has been done.'

Oh, I wouldn't say that was me being lucky that she didn't break a leg.

'So, doing a spot of shopping I see?' I point to all the bags. I know asking her a question is a big mistake. It might infer that I actually want to talk to her. But I feel obliged to make some sort of conversation after spilling her across the pavement.

She frowns curtly at me. Now, that's the look I'm used to. She holds up her bags at me and I swear one of them says Art of Lingerie on it. I try to get a better look but she clocks me and quickly gathers the bags behind her.

'You don't say. Is it all the shopping bags that gave me away?' She then gives a haughty sniff, 'Paul is taking me out tonight, so I need a new dress.'

'Oh, is this for a special occasion?' It's only polite to ask. Damn my mother for teaching me manners.

'Why would you think it has to be a special occasion?' Delilah would be looking down her nose at me right now if I wasn't so much taller than her. 'Peter and moi don't need a special occasion to dine out. Couples don't. Ahh, but then you wouldn't know that, would you?' Delilah pushes out her bottom lip in a fake sad face. It's all I can do to keep a smile stuck on mine.

'But since you asked, yes. Paul is taking me out tonight for our fifth anniversary.' She's looking expectantly at me and so I force out the standard response.

'Congrat...cough cough...ulations.' Yes, folks, that was me choking on a word.

'Hopefully if we manage to hook you up with someone, you too might get to experience an anniversary.' And there it is. Always, always, always. She has to find some way to show off that she's in a relationship and I'm not. However, she will not blot out the sunrays of my day and I will not let her smug smile get to me. As tight as my smile is getting, darn it, it will not be moved from my face!

'Hmm...did you think it could be that zit you got the other day why none of your numerous dates have been successful yet? It WAS huge...' Delilah now gives me a fake sympathetic look. And it was not a big zit. It was a tiny pimple that no one other than Delilah could have noticed in the first place.

A couple of workmen in overalls and hard hats walk towards.

'Hey, sexy lady.' One winks at me and the other takes off his hard hat and gives a little bow. The first one that winked at me then looks at Delilah. She straightens up, ready to receive a compliment.

'You've got a ladder in your tights ma'am. Just thought you should know.' He points to the ladder with a serious expression. Delilah goes bright red and I can't think of a shade that suits her more! The man then turns to me again.

'You have a great day, now.' He says with another wink and he and his friend both continue up the street. Delilah is seething.

'I can't believe he called me ma'am' she mutters under her breath

'He was quite complimentary to me. So I would say no, my *tiny pimple* isn't to blame for anything.' From a tight smile to a smug smile. My day just got great again! Delilah couldn't kill me more with her look if she tried. It reminds me that I did knock her over, and most importantly she is one of the people entrusted to help me find a guy to help me lose something else. I should really, really, *really* try harder to be nicer.

'So where is Paul anyway? I would have thought he would be up here with you?' As in he is never far from your side like a good little Pekinese. Okay, I maybe should add another "really" to me trying harder. It's just "really x 100" hard to do that. I think maybe Delilah is conceding that she should be a little nicer too. I'm her regular ticket to Mum's delightful delicacies at the moment. She takes a deep breath before answering in a significantly less smarmy tone.

'He just popped into one of the shops to pick up some jeans he pre-ordered. I was just on my way to meet him.'

And as if he heard he was being summonsed, here is Paul walk/running up the street to meet his beloved with a similar amount of bags that also seem to be Delilah's from the shop names on them.

'Got them sweetheart. We're all set.' Paul stops in front of Delilah with a big smile which seems to turn into an even wider soppy grin as he notices me.

'Oh! Hi Gina.' He says in a dreamy tone.

'Hello Paul. How are you.' I say with a genuine smile. He's actually quite a nice guy who unfortunately has a not-so-nice girlfriend.

'Goooood. I'm goooood.' Paul's cheeks suddenly start to go pink. Delayed flush from his walk/running to do Delilah's bidding?

'Did you get the shirt with the stripes like I told you?' Delilah is rummaging around in one of Paul's bags.

'Yes, Dee' Paul says absently still staring at me.

'Paul. Why did you get this red one too?

'I like the plain one Dee.'

'Yes, but you know bright colours wash you out.' Delilah has pulled a ghastly red shirt out the bag. For once, I totally agree with her, 'I really think you should change it, babe.' Delilah shoves the shirt back in the bag.

'Yes Dee.'

'And did you confirm with Tia that we can do dinner. I know that so-called boyfriend Gary has been giving her grief again and she needs some support.'

'Yes Dee.' Paul is now looking at me with a dopey smile on his face. A little disconcerting, I might add.

'Oh, and you didn't cancel the order for Mum did you? She's changed her mind again.'

'Yes Dee.' Paul looks like he's floating on a cloud right now as he answers Delilah with his eyes still fixed on me.

'What do you mean yes? I told you not to...' Delilah looks up to see Paul all doe-eyed and not because he's staring at her. She gives him a humungous elbow in the ribs.

'Oooof!' Paul doubles over as Delilah knocks all the wind out of him. I cringe as I can only imagine how much *that* hurt.

'Oops.' Delilah says sweetly, as if you can accidentally elbow someone in the rib cage.

'Anyway, we must dash – to get ready for our *anniversary* dinner.' Delilah emphasises anniversary for both mine and Paul's benefit. She's back to that smarmy look again, like it's my fault her boyfriend stares at me like he's high. Tch.

'Oh yes, before I forget. Tell Lisa that Oliver called and everything is a go. He'll be back in time, so the provisional booking is now confirmed. Now, I've gone to a lot of trouble to arrange this so you'd better *not* mess it up, like you usually seem to do.' Delilah flicks her hair haughtily and it takes my last ounce of strength to not tug what is obviously extensions.

'Now, I've already allowed you to take up far too much of my time.' Delilah links her arm through Paul's who still seems to be catching his breath from the jolt in his ribs, 'Bye.' And with that, she strides down the road pulling Paul along with her. Wow. The original Delilah may have cut off the hair on Samson's head, but this domineering Delilah has definitely cut something else off of Paul.

Right. That was twenty minutes of my life I'll never get back, and all because I wasn't looking where I was going. If that isn't a lesson in itself, I don't know what is. Right now, I am going to get back to enjoying my day because somewhere out there – in Mr Shah's delicatessen – there is a melted cheese Panini with my name written on it.

Twenty Five

'Hmm Gina, I'm not sure how good a sign it is when it takes this long to find you a partner. Me and Paul hit it off on the first date, within the first hour. And we're still hitting it off 5 years later as you saw for yourself the other day when you met us on our *anniversary*.' Why does the Not-so-delightful Delilah feel she has to emphasise that word every time she uses it in my presence?

'Can it really be everyone else that's the problem?' Delilah gives an innocent look while eating a slice of Mum's Red Velvet Surprise. I hope the surprise is that she chokes on it. Sorry, that sounds a little harsh. If the surprise is that she puts on a stone, I could live with that too.

'Yes Delilah it can,' Lisa says dismissively, 'Because it's much easier to spot a dork these days, than it was when say, you were dating.'

If looks could kill Delilah would murder my friend in a similar way to how she's murdering that slice of cake. I love Lisa!

'Okay everyone, here we are again. Before we start, has everyone got their raffle tickets for the draw?'

Everyone – except me – pulls out a pink stub.

'I'm feeling lucky, Henry; my palm has been itching all week.' Mum is waving her ticket with glee. 'Remember the last time I said my palm felt itchy and then we won an extra portion of chicken wings at Mr Shah's Chicken Shack?' Dad shrugs his shoulders and shows Mum his ticket which she proceeds to blow upon for good luck.

'Gina, would you like to do the honours?' Lisa shakes a muslin bag at me.

'Erm...you guys are having a raffle?'

'Patsy thought it would be a good idea. To add a bit of spice to coming to these meetings every week.'

'Not that helping you isn't reason enough, boss!' Patsy interjects with a nervous smile. Why can't she think of these bright ideas when she's at the shop is what I want to know. I mean, I could raffle a lingerie set as the prize and...

'Ahem?' Lisa shakes the bag at me again to get my attention. I reluctantly walk over and dip my hand in the bag.

'What's the prize anyway?'

'A set of lingerie from the Racy Rouge range from your shop.'

I glare at Patsy who mouths at me from across the room 'It was last season's so I didn't think you'd mind.' I don't mind for once. That's actually not a bad idea to offload some old stock. I do believe Patsy may have stumbled onto a good idea for when we're in between sales and have still got old stock...my train of thought is interrupted again as Lisa shakes the bag with my hand still in it. I withdraw both my hand and a ticket.

'Number 48'

'Yes!' Mum pounds the air with her fist, 'Henry, that's your prize tonight too.' She wiggles her eyebrows at Dad who rubs his hands together and has a crazed sort of grin on his face.

'Eew!' Me and Cousin Mona both cry at the same time.

'Mum, Dad, Please. Too much information' I cringe with embarrassment.

'Definitely T.M.I. Auntie Joan.' Cousin Mona shakes her head and starts texting on her phone.

Mum shrugs her shoulders and passes Dad a slice of the Red Velvet Surprise. I don't need three guesses as to what his surprise is going to be. Ugh, I don't even need one guess.

'Okay folks, now the raffle is over let's get to the meeting at hand. I would like to select the next candidate for Gina to date.'

My eyes open in surprise. There aren't many people Lisa knows that I don't – we have been friends most of our lives. Most of the men she knows are really not the kind of guys I want to even attempt telling my secret to.

'His name is Jackson and he's a Taekwondo Master. He teaches the advanced class at my fighting school. He is also an action stunt double and has worked all over the world. We all call him Action.'

'That's a cool nickname considering what he does.' Cousin Mona looks up from her phone, impressed enough to stop mid text.

'Oh it's not a nickname, that's his *actual* name. He changed it by deed poll when he won his second black belt.'

'How interesting. Shall we say.' Delilah smirks behind another bite of Mum's cake. Oh, for a crumb to slip down her windpipe...

'Ooh, has he been in any good movies? Was he in that Crouching Tiger film? Or Die Hard?' I think they may be the names of the only two movies Mum has seen with an element of fighting in.

'No, I don't think so Mrs Robbins, but he was in nearly all the fight scenes in Night of The Warrior.'

'Oh...I don't think I've heard of that one?' Mum looks at Dad who shrugs his shoulders.

'I think it may have gone straight to DVD.' Lisa takes a bite of the Red Velvet Surprise Mum has just handed her.

'In any case, how exciting. Isn't that exciting Henry? Just think, there might be an actor in the family soon.' Mum clasps her hands to her heart as if she's practising to audition in front of him.

'Yes dear, very exciting.' Dad acknowledges as he turns the page of my latest edition of Cosmopolitan.

'It's hardly that exciting. Paul could have been an actor in college – he nearly got cast in Home Alone as one of the brothers but instead, he opted for a more steady profession as a retail assistant.' Delilah mumbles under her breath.

'So, this Jackson is a fighter? He must be well fit!' There's not much that can peak Cousin

Mona's interest enough to take her attention away from her phone.

'Yes, he is very physically fit – he has abs to die for.' Lisa's eyes glaze over for a moment as if she's reminiscing on Jackson's six pack. As I survey the room, I see all the ladies with a similar look in their eyes – even Gran!

'And he's 6ft 2 with thick juicy lips.' Lisa continues to a harmonised chorus of sighs from all the females in the room. I only just manage to suppress a sigh of my own – he really does sound super fine.

'Have you got a picture of this Action person?' Delilah asks nonchalantly but I can see in the whites of her eyes it's not for my benefit she wants to view this fellow.

'Sure.' Lisa reaches into her bag and all the women rush over to her, Delilah moves a little slower so as not to show her eagerness, but the determination in her step isn't fooling anyone. The picture must clearly do him justice.

'Ooh...' says Mum
'Raaah...' says Patsy
'Cor!' says Cousin Mona
'Hmph' says Delilah
'Wow...' says Gran.

'Yeah...' says Lisa

Dad just rolls his eyes and Mr Shah starts standing noticeably straighter and I'm sure he's holding in his stomach.

'Do you want to see his picture, Gina?' Lisa asks me

'I think I can wait.' I say calmly, but it is taking all my willpower to keep my tail in my seat and not sprint over to join them.

'Okay then. Back to the matter at hand. I know Rymans bar is not your place of choice for dates anymore Gina, so can anyone suggest...'

'No! Rymans is fine.' After that fight scene at the Seniors Club I will be more than happy with the familiarity of Rymans. There's no chance of snarling bag-wielding pensioners raging towards me there. I still wake up in a cold sweat at the memory.

'Oh really? That's great then! He actually takes an evening class down the road from there so he can just come straight after. Plus, Rymans are introducing double happy hour from 7.00 to 9.00 pm every Tuesday now to encourage more business on their slow night. I'll sort out a table for you so you guys can have some nibbles too. Action has never been to Rymans so you can give him the grand tour.'

Sure, I mean there's so much to see. I can show him the bar, the lobby and the men's toilets with original urinals from The Bathroom Centre.

'Do you think Jackson could get us free tickets for his next movie?' Cousin Mona perks up from behind her phone, 'It would so help my cred in the Students Lounge.'

'I'm sure Gina can ask on her next date' the sarcasm drips from Delilah's tongue as she dramatically flicks the magazine page.

'No Gina cannot.' Bloomin' cheek! 'And on that note, I believe today's meeting is adjourned so I bid you all a good evening.'

Everyone starts making moves to leave. Lisa looks a little peeved because that's usually her thing to end the meeting. Still, she clips her pencil against her clip board before shoving it in her oversized bag and joining the end of the queue of everyone leaving.

I start picking up plates and glasses as I shoo everyone out the door. Before I can close it, Lisa pops her head back through and puts her little finger and thumb to her ear and mouth.

'Call me!'

I give one big nod and close the door firmly behind her. As I rest my forehead against the door, I realise that I'm really warming to the idea of meeting someone for real. I'm going to get over this virgin hurdle if it kills me and the way it's going so far it just might.

Twenty Six

I'm actually quite glad the date has been arranged at Rymans tonight. I don't know if it's the location, the half price cocktails or the fact that I've been here so many times in the last few weeks why I feel so comfortable here.

It's a fairly busy night tonight – busier than usual for a Tuesday. The double happy hour promotion must be working. Lisa suggested we go for a pink carnation to identify one another like the date with Stu with the white carnation. I agreed without hesitation as that idea is infinitely better than the airport sign that Gregory the food teacher used on our date, not to mention less conspicuous.

I go straight to the bar to order and take advantage of the new double happy hour rule. I need a little dutch courage tonight so there's no point in me paying more for it than I have to. I barely take a sip from my Virgin Mary cocktail – my now signature drink for obvious reasons – when I get a tap on the shoulder.

'Fancy seeing you here.'

I twirl slowly on the bar stool, 'Jess? Jessica Montrose?' I jump off the stool and we both hug and jump and squeal like two little piglets!

'Oh my gosh, how long has it been?' I wrack my brains to remember.

'Melinda's housewarming party when she moved into Bourneville Street!'

'That's right!' I concur and we jump and squeal a bit more.

'So, what on earth are you doing here? Are you here with Bobby?' I ask after I've caught my breath. Winded after a few jumps – I really need to get my jogging on.

'Well, it really has been too long.' Jess screws up her face a little, 'Me and Bobby aren't together now.'

'I can see that. Is it his turn to shop while you have a daiquiri and wait for him?' I smile knowingly.

'No...I mean we've split up.'

'Jess, I totally get it. It makes sense to both go where you want and meet up again afterwards. I mean who really wants to be hanging around in men's shops looking at belts?' I give her an exaggerated wink and nod.

'Nooo Gina. I mean me and Bobby are no longer a couple.'

'What? What are you talking about? Stop playing.' I give her a playful punch.

Jess shakes her head at me solemnly, 'Not playing.'

I look hard at my friend waiting for the punch line that isn't coming. Jessica and Bobby have been together since we were all at school. It's always been in the back of my mind that if I ever popped my tart (one of Lisa's expressions that has unfortunately imprinted itself on my mind), I'd want a relationship just like theirs – all committed and forever after. I haven't even put the pop tart in the toaster and already I have to think about remodelling the relationship I'm not even in yet. I mean, if Jess and Bobby couldn't make it as non-virgins, what chance did I have?

'What on earth happened? Or is that a story for another day?'

'It's definitely the latter. It's a tale where one girl and three guys isn't as much fun as it might sound.'

'No way!' My toes are literally curling with interest.

'Yes way! I could write a book about it.' Jess laughs and I guess I'm relieved that she seems okay about whatever happened. Her laugh also reminds me how much fun we used to have back in college.

'Okay, then we need to catch up *real* soon! Because this story I need to hear.' I don't mention that it will also be a welcome distraction from my own dating life woes.

'We will definitely. I'll call you to arrange something. I only really popped in here to meet Tyrone to drop off the spare set of keys. He locked his set in the house.'

'Tyrone?'

'Yes, Ty-rone...' Jess emphasises the Ty and the Rone and gives me a penetrating stare as if willing something into my mind. Then suddenly it hits me.

'Hey, that's not the Tyrone from...'

'Yep, the very same.' Jess interrupts me.

'Right. The time frame has now moved. You need to call me before the week is out!' I tug on her hair to remind her. A neuro linguistic programming technique I learnt from Lisa that she learnt from some program she watches called Don't tell me Lies. I've even watched a few episodes myself and memorised a few expressions. In fact, I saw Cousin Mona with one of them exact looks on her face last week when I asked her to help me stock take. She actually lied about having to stay late at Uni! I was more excited I was right than upset to be honest. Anyway, now when Jess touches her hair she'll remember to call.

'I definitely will. Tyrone is clearly not here and I need to pick up Martell from Taekwondo. Oh Gina, his teacher is a hunk of gorgeousness called Mr Jackson. I tell you, if I didn't love that man of mine.' Jess fans herself to emphasise just how hot this guy is. Hold on...could it really be...

'Hey, do people call this teacher Action?'

'Yeah, and I'm sure most of the Mums stay to watch their kids take the class just to see him. Hey, you're always single. I could defo get you guys hooked up!' Jess looks like she's stumbled upon the meaning of life, she looks so excited at the prospect of finding a date for me. It's like a contagious disease that everyone around me wants to find me dates!

'I'm actually meeting someone this evening. That's why I'm here.' I smile calmly at her but really I'm itching to tell her that I'm going to be on a date with the same guy in about ten minutes! She'll want to ask me twenty questions about how I met him and so on, then she'll be late to pick up her child and before you know it, Social Services will be serving her with an ASBO for being an unfit mother or something. In any case, I can't have her losing custody of her only son on my conscience so I'll save telling her about my date with all the Taekwondo Mum's dreamboat when we speak later in the week.

'I'd be tempted to stick around and shake this mystery date's hand for getting this far if I didn't have to dash. Martell will be non-stop whining if he doesn't see me the minute he exits that class.' Jess strokes her hair as she pushes away her stool.

'But I will call you before the week's out – see, I haven't forgotten!'

I am so putting Don't tell me Lies on series link when I get in! As Jess rushes towards the door she looks back to wag a finger at me.

'And I want to hear all about this date when I call, none of your crazy excuses as to why it didn't work out!'

Geez, what's her name? Lisa? As she gets to the exit she blows me a kiss and gives me the

I'll-call-you sign with her thumb and little finger which makes her miss the opening and spin twice in the revolving door. I *knew* it was the stupid door and not me! Where's that bloomin' Dave now? Trust him to only be around when these things happen to me. Jess smacks herself on the forehead as she properly exits the second time and gives me a final wave goodbye.

I turn back towards the bar on my stool to get the barman's attention but he is already in front of me with a Virgin Mary and a big wink. I reach for the fancy glass and start sipping. It's not long before I get another tap on my shoulder. I twirl on the stool again – I'm getting quite good at this – and am faced with the broadest chest I've ever seen. I slowly look up...and up...and up – this guy must be just short of seven foot tall. And right there, looking like a pink spot in the middle of his chest is a carnation.

'Gina? I'm Jackson. Lisa's friend.'

His voice is so deep, it feels like my ears are vibrating. This Hercules is in Lisa's Taekwondo class? And teaches Jess's kid? And he's single? This is like a Twilight zone moment.

'You *are* Gina, right?' He looks a little unsure and that's when I realise I haven't answered him yet due to my tongue still hanging out of my mouth.

'Yes! Yes, I'm Gina. Pleased to meet you.'

'Phew, I wasn't sure if it was you. I saw you talking to your friend and it looked like a regular girls night – no men allowed.'

'Oh, ha ha, that's my college friend that I haven't seen in a while. We were squeezing in a catch up session.' I smile and his response is just to stare at me.

'Is everything okay?'

'Sorry! Lisa undersold just how good looking you are.'

This direct compliment makes me blush like I've never blushed before. Now I truly understand what everyone was getting excited about. He is just too-much-good-looking for one man. A mirror would tell Brad Pitt (the Ocean's 11 version) to get out of the way if this Action man was standing behind him, *that* is how hot he is.

'Oh thanks. Thank you.' I can't help but flush a little. He has these sexy slitty eyes that look like he's staring at you intensely all the time. I feel I could just sink into them if I stare into them long enough. I shake myself out of the hypnotic state I'm in and back to reality.

'Sorry, I ordered myself a drink while I was waiting.' In truth, I didn't need to because as soon as I sat down the bar man put it in front of me – but he doesn't need to know that.

'No worries, I'll just get myself a beer.' He indicates to the bar man to bring him a bottle. His eyes light up and he gives me a devastating smile. Oh, to be the top of that bottle right now. Jackson sits on the stool next to me making it look like a child's seat. I actually think he might be balancing one bum cheek on it. Oh, to be that stool right now.

'Chairs are a little on the small side.' He moves uncomfortably but still manages to keep that super smile on his face. I can see not a lot of conversation will be going on if he has to balance like that for a few hours. How sorry do I feel for what I can clearly imagine must be a perfect bum cheek.

'If you're hungry we can go over to the eating area? Or they have a few slouchy sofas where we can chill?' Rymans has a surprising amount of nooks to relax in if you just want to chat.

'A slouchy sofa sounds great. I don't usually like to eat straight after a class. Adrenalin still pumping, you know.'

Really? After teaching kids?

'My friend has a son who does Taekwondo. His name is Martell?'

'Oh yes, young Martell. He has a lot of potential.'

Jackson tells me a little more about Martell's budding skills as the bar man gives him a bottle of beer which he promptly wrenches the cap off with his teeth. His bare, perfectly straight, totally lickable teeth. And on top of that, he did it in slow motion, or that's what it looked like to me.

I grab my Mary and we walk over to one of the slouchy sofas. I drop into the seat first with Jackson going for the seat opposite me. He made the stool look tiny and unfortunately, the sofa is no better. He sinks to the bottom of it like it's made of sponge.

'Erm, maybe the slouchy sofa wasn't that great an idea after all.' Jackson laughs showing all those perfectly shaped perfectly white teeth. I easily vacate my seat to help dislodge Jackson from the seat which turns out to be tricky. Not because all I can concentrate on are his solid biceps between my fingers, but because he's as heavy as he looks and for all my efforts, this dude is not budging. A man sitting a sofa down canoodling his girlfriend sees me huffing and puffing and jumps up.

'I'll give you a hand, love.' He gives me a big smile and takes Jackson's arm from me. I note the smile is not shared by his girlfriend, which I find surprising. I mean he's being chivalrous which is a rare quality these days. She should be proud she has a man who'll offer to help someone in distress. Another guy jumps up leaving his girlfriend holding her glass in the air that she was just about to offer him a sip from. Guy 2 kind of nudges Guy 1 out of the way and takes Jackson's other arm.

'I think I can be of more assistance to the lady.' Guy 2 gives me a beaming smile too.

Guy 1 gives Guy 2 a pointed look, 'Thanks for the offer, but I've got this.'

Guy 2 points his finger in Guy 1's face, 'What you *should* be getting is back to your lady friend over there and leave this to someone who can handle it.' Guy 2 then nods at me with a big wink.

Guy 1 grits his teeth and tugs Jackson's arm towards him, 'Don't worry about my lady, your one over there looks like she needs the attention.' I look over, and indeed, Guy 2's girlfriend is still holding the glass aloft with screwed up eyes and a pout on her lips.

Guy 2 gives me another wink, then gives his girl a wink – I'm starting to wonder if he has something in his eye, 'My girl will get all the attention she can handle, as soon as I've helped this sweet thing out with her friend.'

Guy 1 starts to yank Jackson's arm to pull him out of the chair, 'I said I've got this!'

Guy 2 is now pulling vigorously too with poor Jackson looking from one guy to the other wondering no doubt what the heck is going on. The two girlfriends are looking daggers at me like I had something to do with this!

'Erm, gentlemen...' Before I can utter a further word, both turn to me and say 'Yes?' with straightened backs and macho faces.

'My friend?' I point to Jackson who is struggling to help himself out of the sofa and failing abysmally – through no fault of his own really as his arms *are* being controlled by other people. Both men sort of mumble apologies to me (I'm not sure why they're apologising to me, I'm not the one stuck in the seat with my arms being yanked off!) and then start to co-ordinate their efforts to help Jackson. With an almighty heave, they manage to extricate him out of the seat. He shakes both guys hands and slaps them on the back. They both fall forward under the force, but quickly straighten up. Guy 1 rolls his shoulders forward as if to say 'It's nothing, I'm okay' while Guy 2 quickly smoothes back his hair as if to say, 'It's all good, I'm okay.'

'I think maybe I could tackle a little something after that. Shall we eat?' Jackson shakes his legs out and places his hand in the small of my back.

'Sure.' I say. I turn to both guys, 'Thanks for your help, fellas.'

It's like they both sort of go woozy in front of me while looking totally flush-faced as they say 'No problem' and 'Anytime' respectively. I guess helping Jackson took a little more out of them than they anticipated – he is a giant of a man after all.

As Guy 2 walks back towards his girl, flexing his shoulders at his good deed, she "accidentally" spills the wine she was meant to feed him moments ago into his lap. Guy 1's girl gives him a whack with her purse when he attempts to start canoodling where he left off. Actually, that whack brings back a fleeting vision of my near handbag attack at Gran's Seniors club. I quickly shudder the memory away.

'Are you okay?' Jackson is resting both his hands on my shoulders and looking down on me in concern. I mean *literally* looking down on me.

Did I mention already that he is about 7-foot tree? (yes, I did mean 7-foot T-R-E-E not three).

I am tempted to just stay for a little while longer basking in the glory of his palms but I remember it's a date where I've got to make my revelation. It was so much easier when I was preparing to fail these dates rather than succeed in them. And I really wouldn't mind if this hunk of man-ness is the one I succeed with. How would *that* be for my very first catch!

'Yes, I'm fine!' I smile as I zone back into the present. 'I think I'm a little peckish now too.'

We walk over to the food area and start looking for the reserve sign where Lisa has pre-reserved us a table, when the usual serving waiter beckons to us and points to a table beside him. Not before I see him accidentally barge another lady out of the way when she attempted to sit there.

'Ahh, Miss Gina. So lovely to see you again so soon. Miss Lisa reserved a table for you, but that buffoon Maurice chose one that was inferior to what you deserve. I believe this one would be more fitting to one such as you. And of course, your friend.' The waiter gives me a little bow and hands both me and Jackson a menu. This is new, as he usually ignores whoever I'm with. Then again, Jackson *is* hard to ignore – by anyone.

'I think I'll just have a few barbecue wings.' As I make my choice I immediately want to retract it. I mean, gnawing meat straight off the bone with my hands? In front of this guy? What am I thinking!

'Good choice. But I think I'll go with a quarter pound burger.' Geez, he even makes a burger sound like a real man's food. Jackson smiles a thank you at the waiter and even he seems to be mesmerised by it. As we settle into our seats and the waiter speeds off to fulfil our orders, Jackson is doing that staring thing again.

'What?' I ask quickly, more to throw him off the fact that I've been doing the exact same thing to him.

'I'm just finding it hard to believe that Lisa has a single friend that looks like you.' Ditto.

'So, what do you do, Gina?'

'I sell women's lingerie.' I take a sip of my cocktail. It's had as much adventure as me so far tonight.

'Okay, now there's no way that a woman that looks like you and sells sexy underwear should not be snapped up unless you have some kind of secret.'

I choke on my Mary as he says this and cough most of the liquid up through my nose. I look at him wide-eyed as he continues.

'It's the only thing that makes sense. I mean, look at you?' Jackson looks at me in disbelief and shakes his head, 'So? What is it?'

'Hmm? What is what?' I say innocently, wiping excess cocktail off my cheek.

'What is this secret you're hiding for why you're still single?' He's giving me that disarming smile again. Okay, I wasn't expecting this line of questioning so soon. I thought he'd at least lead with "How long have you known Lisa?" and then maybe touch on "What movies have you seen lately?" before getting on to why I am still single. I can feel myself panicking. I wasn't prepared to deal with this straight away! Now my game plan has changed, I need to warm up to these things. I need more time and nothing buys you time like a trip to the loo. But before I can excuse myself, Jackson beats me to it.

Twenty Seven

'Hold that answer! I've really got to go take a leak. I religiously have 2 litres of water after a class and it seems to have made its way through me sooner than expected.' Jackson squeezes my hand as he leaves the table and my legs turn to jelly. There's no way I can make it to the ladies on these pins after that. As I take this breather to think of how I'm going to broach his yet unanswered question, the conversation from the table just behind me catches my attention. I manoeuvre myself to an angle so I can see the couple out of the corner of my eye.

'Come on Sarah, this is our third date. No one waits this long anymore.' Creepy guy appears to be nuzzling up against this Sarah girl's cheek, who doesn't seem to be liking it as much as he is.

'Johnny, I'm just not sure.' Sarah gives him a wistful look

'What's there to be sure about? Everybody our age is doing it now, so why wait? It's the norm.'

'Really?' Sarah now gives him an unsure look. I'm quite surprised at how well I can see from the corner of my eye. I adjust a little more just the same because if I stay like this much longer, I'll have a crooked neck for sure.

'Of course. Absolutely. And guys will not hang around waiting for you when they can just get it as the *norm* from the next girl in the room.' The worldly look he gives Sarah would actually convince even me...okay, well maybe not. I *am* nearly (cough cough) her age.

'Oh...they won't?'

'Nope. They will not. I'm not trying to force you - I would never do that, I like you too much. I'm just trying to prepare you.'

Ugh, that has got to be the sickliest sweet smile I've ever seen a guy give a girl. Hmm...actually, a close second sickliest. Limp haired Leslie had the super sickliest smile I've ever seen when he asked me to go out one Valentines just before the fight he had with Toby in Mr Shah's mini supermarket. I think I told him that seeing too many red hearts made the blood rush to my head. What? Well, I thought it was a pretty good excuse at the time, and it worked because he sent smelling salts to my workplace the following year on Valentines.

'Oh...I didn't know that...' I can hear Sarah's resolve crumbling by the second.

'When you think about it, I would actually be doing you a favour. Guys usually run a mile from girls like you.' Johnny double raises his eyebrows. What does he mean "girls like her"?

'What do you mean - girls like me?'

Wow, how in tune am I with this girl that we're even thinking the same questions. Or maybe I read it in her expression. I've watched quite a few ad hoc episodes of Don't Tell Me Lies lately. I feel like quite the expert.

'You know. Girls that haven't done it before. Virgins. Guys want experienced girls and I'm willing to help you get that experience.'

'But I could get pregnant and my mum would kill me!' Sarah says earnestly.

'Nonsense. That just doesn't happen when you do it for the first time.'

Okay, that's it! I have eavesdropped enough. I can't sit here for another second listening to this moron try and convince this girl that if she wants to be accepted she has to give it up and then lie to her about possibly getting pregnant to boot!

But I can't just butt in can I? It's not like we're in the ladies loo where it's a given to inveigle yourself into other women's conversations. Still, I need to find a way to tell her not to be taken in by this guy. But how? And then the craziest of ideas hits me. I look around to make sure no-one is watching me. I don't count the two waiters, the bar man or that greasy-haired man in the corner because they are more looking at me – as in my person rather than watching me – as in my actions. I know it may sound the same, but it's really not.

Anyway, I get up and walk past their table humming to myself a little so that they think I'm totally uninterested in their conversation. Then I suddenly shout, 'No way! It can't be...!' and point across the room. When the couple, plus the two waiters, the bar man and the greasy haired man in the corner all stare in the direction where I'm pointing, I grab the mobile phone on the table next to Sarah, hide it behind my back and keep walking until I get to the big potted plant near the revolving exit door. I'm praying that this Sarah girl is like me and hasn't put a lock on her phone. I swipe the screen and the date and a screensaver of a scruffy looking Yorkshire terrier pops up. I quickly go to the phone screen, tap out my number and call my phone so that her number registers on it. Okay, now to get the phone back before it's missed.

As I walk back to my seat and pass the couple's table again, I point in the same direction again, 'Oh my gosh, it really is!' Everyone looks in the direction I'm pointing again. As I go to quickly put the phone back, in my haste it hits the side of the table and clatters onto the floor. The eating area goes quiet and both Sarah, Johnny, the two waiters, the bar man and the greasy haired man in the corner are now all watching me (not looking – see the difference now?).

I quickly bend down to pick up the phone, 'Sorry. I thought I saw Idris Elba.' Sarah quickly cranes her neck to look around again, just to be sure my mistake *was* a mistake – even I look in the direction that she's looking, just to be doubly sure.

'Luckily no damage done, phew!' I mock wipe my brow as I hand her back her phone. Sarah smiles at me then gives me a confused look as I nod and give her a big wink before going back to my table. Johnny the rat has barely waited for my departure before he starts trying to wear down Sarah's resolve a little more. Well, we'll soon see about that. I quickly text a message to the missed call number showing on my phone.

`Stay strong.`

I hear Sarah's phone vibrate and out of the corner of my eye, I see her pick it up, read the message and look around before placing her phone back onto the table. I quickly tap out another text message to her

`Don't let this Dick make you think you have to take his Dick just so everybody will like you.`

I see her eyes widen in surprise and she looks around to her left and right to see where the messages are coming from. She then taps the phone screen and turns the machine around in her hand staring hard at it. I'm guessing to make sure the phone isn't maybe a magic phone that just sends messages to itself?

'Everything okay babe?' Johnny takes a swig of his coke.

'Err...yeah. I'm fine.' Sarah shakes her head to concentrate on what the idiot in front of her is telling her.

'As I was saying, I'd actually be helping you out. That kind of makes me a good guy.' Johnny points his glass of coke at Sarah as if to emphasise the point. I send another text.

```
Not a good guy! More like a bad
liar!
```

I see Sarah pick up her phone again and look around. But this time, something else happens.

'Are you sure that's true?' Sarah says quietly after reading the message.

'Is what true babe?'

'That you'd be doing me a favour?'

'Of course! What you've got to remember is that there aren't many girls like you around.'

I quickly text again.

```
That makes you special and
rare. To be valued. Like a blood
red ruby!
```

I hear Sarah repeat, 'That would rarely make me special like a Ruby then.'

'Huh?' Johnny looks at Sarah strangely who quickly looks down at her phone again.

'What I mean is that would make me rare and special if there aren't a lot of girls like me. Like a bloody ruby that's red. Wouldn't it?'

Johnny is stuck for words for a few seconds.

'Erm...well...of course you are babe. Especially when you put it like that. But you don't want to be so different from everyone else that people think you're weird.' Johnny sure can make a quick recovery. Luckily, I've heard that one before – well, technically it was an exchange I had with myself when I went over all the possible reactions I would get if I told anyone my secret – in any case, I know just the right response for that and quickly tap it out and press send.

```
Why would you be weird because
you don't want to take your
knickers off to the first pleb
that asks you?
```

I see Sarah concentrating on reading the text and start to bite her lip. Me thinks maybe that's a little too direct for her to repeat. I quickly tap out another message.

```
Why is not being ready weird?
```

I see the relief in her eyes out of the corner of mine as she reads the new message.

'Why is it strange if I'd want to wait?' Sarah says calmly. I think now she's getting the *message* from the messages. Johnny is staring at her a little suspiciously now.

'What you looking at on your phone babe?'

'Oh, that's just a friend messaging me. As I was saying, why is it weird that I'm not ready?' Sarah sounds a little forceful now. Good for her!

'Because guys can take their pick of girls out there that *are* ready *and* willing to do it at the drop of a hat. So you should be too if you want to be considered normal. I'm just saying.' Johnny shrugs his shoulders innocently. The look on his face all fake concern. Ooh, I'd like to...okay, stay calm Gina.

'Really? All the girls are doing it? *Already?*'

'Yes babe. Like it's a new dance.'

'So I'm the only one not doing it then?' Sarah looks like she's starting to fall for his crap again. I start to text rapidly.

`You are not! Trust me there are plenty of other females around just like you and twice your age!`

Sarah looks shocked as she reads my text. Not as shocked as I am at myself for actually putting something like that in writing! Okay, time to try a different tact. I don't want her to end up waiting as long as me to lose hers but I'll be damned if I'm going to sit and watch some creep trying to trick her into giving it up like it's a freebie in a super-market offer. I quickly tap out another message.

`Tell him this: I need to think about it.`

Sarah repeats what I text. Two seconds later I send the next one.

`I've thought about it and I want to wait. But if you want`

`to go to one of those girls that`
`are happy not to, I understand.`

Then a piece de resistance suddenly unfolds. Sarah doesn't wait for another text but goes full on ad lib!

'And what's more, I heard that if a woman isn't absolutely ready to have sex, that when a man enters her, the vagina will clamp down onto his dick like a vice to protect itself. Do you know what a vice is, Johnny?' Sarah leans forward to glare into Johnny's eyes whose jaw drops in shock at what he's just heard. He then jumps up and scrapes his chair back as he realises he's spilt his coke into his own lap!

'I just wouldn't want mine to do that to you, Johnny.' Sarah puts on a mock concern face.

You go girl! I feel like a proud Mama. I couldn't have written that response better myself. I think my work is done here. I quickly tap out a final message:

`Now   excuse   yourself   and   go`
`home.`

I hear Sarah repeat my message, word for word including 'I am excusing myself and going home,'...but she's still sitting down staring at her phone. I text her again.

Erm...you're supposed to get up and leave.Now!

Sarah nods at the phone and gets up and walks out to Johnny's shocked expression. Two minutes later, he is running out after her and five minutes after that, I get a ping on my phone. It's a text from Sarah.

He said he was just joking and will wait for as long as I want! Thank you! Whoever you are!

I lean back in my chair with a satisfied smile to a job well done, if I do say so myself. I feel like a super hero – saving the innocent lambs from the wolves who would take advantage of them. Maybe this is the real reason why my potato hasn't yet been roasted. Still beaming, I look at my watch – Jackson has really been gone a while.

I'm so elated, I think I'll give a quick call to Lisa and tell her how I saved someone's virginity. It's as if she was waiting for my call, she answers so quickly.

'Oh no, what's happened?' Lisa groans down the phone.

'Oh, nothing yet – Jackson is still in the loo.'

'What do you mean he's still in the loo?'

'Never mind that, I had to tell you how I saved someone's virginity!'

'What?' I can just imagine the crease of confusion along Lisa's brow right now.

'Yeah, some creep was trying to persuade his girlfriend that being a virgin was a bad thing, so I helped her to tell him that wasn't the case!'

'What?'

'Yeah, I really did! I texted her what to say and in the end, he backed right off and then she texted me to say he'd wait until she was ready!'

'What?'

'I've got to go now – I think you're right to ask why Jackson is still in the loo because he really has been gone a while. Even a number two shouldn't take this long.'

'What? Ugh!' I can just imagine Lisa wrinkling her nose.

'Call you later!' I hang up quickly and make my way towards the Men's toilets.

Twenty Eight

As I reach the immediate vicinity of the Men's toilets, I start hovering outside the door. I mean, I can hardly just burst straight in there like some toilet groupie can I? I pretend to look at a menu hung on the wall next to the door and it briefly crosses my mind that it's actually a strange place to put a menu. I mean, right beside a toilet? Really?

I cock my head to the side like I'm really concentrating on the list of starters and slyly look to the left, then to the right to make sure the coast is clear before gently pushing the door open. The door is suddenly wrenched open from the other side causing me to jump backwards as a man comes out and gives me a strange look.

'Can I help you love?'

'Erm no, but I think I can help you. Your fly is undone.' I pointedly nod towards his southern area. The man looks down quickly and a red flush tinges his cheeks (his face cheeks, that is) as he grabs for his zipper and practically barges me out of the way.

'You're welcome!' I shout after him. I roll my eyes and gently push the main toilet door open again.

'Hello?' I call. The room appears to be empty and surprisingly cleaner than I would have expected the men's loos to be. In fact, it actually looks cleaner than the women's loo!

'Jackson?' I whisper loudly, 'Jackson? Are you in here?'

'Gina, is that you?'

'Yes! You've been gone a while, so I got a bit concerned. Thought maybe you were stuck or something.' I give a little laugh and turn to make my way back out.

'Well...funny you should say that...' Jackson starts and then goes silent.

'You're not are you? Stuck?'

'Well, actually...' Jackson states again.

I walk along the cubicles pushing the doors until I come to one that does not budge. I knock.

'Jackson?'

'Yes! I'm in a bit of a tight spot, pardon the pun. I didn't realise how small the space with this seat was until I sat down and couldn't get back up.'

Ooh, another difference between men and women revealed – they actually sit on public toilet seats. I don't mind admitting I did not know that.

'I'll go and get some help to get the door open.' I turn to leave.

'No! Erm no. I'd rather you didn't. The manager's son goes to my Taekwondo class. In fact, I've seen the faces of a few parents here so if you don't mind, I'd rather not have any of them come to help and see me like this.' Jackson's voice tapers off to a near whisper.

'Oh...kay. What can I do?'

'Well, a hand would be great.' I could take that to mean so many things right now but I'm gonna go with the kind of hand he was given to help him up from the slouchy sofa earlier.

'Right.' I start thinking of how this is going to work bearing in mind getting outside help to open the door is not an option. I can only come to one conclusion.

'I'm going to have to climb over into your cubicle.'

'That sounds like a plan.' I can hear the relief in his voice that I seem to have come up with an idea that doesn't require any other intervention. I go into the cubicle next door and strangely, the first thought that enters my head is what I'm going to look like clambering into his cubicle. On one hand, I'm lucky I wore a flared skirt so my movement won't be restricted. On the other hand, I would have been luckier if I wore trousers, but who knew I'd be staging a rescue? I roll off some toilet paper and wipe the seat before kicking off my shoes and climbing on top of it. Luckily there's a big gap at the top of the wall between the cubicles. I grasp the top and scramble with my feet against the wall to hoist myself to the top. I know there's no point in trying to fix my skirt, but I do anyway.

I manage to slide over the gap onto the other side of the wall. I'm quite impressed with how easily I've taken to this – maybe obstacle courses are in my future.

'Incoming!' I call to Jackson before losing my grip and landing slap bang into his lap.

'Oomph!' Jackson expels air as I wind him – which also serves as a reminder that I really need to start that diet. I'm just thankful that the air he just let loose didn't come from somewhere else seeing where we are.

'Sorry! Lost my grip!' And broke *another* nail, dammit!

'No worries.' Jackson rasps clearly still breathless. I quickly wriggle out of his lap – which I admit gives me a fleetingly nice feeling - and smooth my hair then rearrange my skirt so that it's back over my knees. Good thing Patsy persuaded me to sample some of the new underwear lines every time I went on a date so that I could advise customers how it made me feel. I can honestly say, I feel really good that I've got some on today.

I face Jackson and immediately see that he makes the toilet seat look like a child's one. A small child's one at that. It's a weird looking toilet seat I must say. There is a kind of frame around the toilet seat that has what looks like...arm rests? I kid you not. Never seen anything like it – it really looks like a 'throne' in all senses of the word and he is well and truly lodged in there. It's not surprising really as it's not even a very big arm chair-type toilet to be in a men's room. Or maybe it just doesn't look very big with him sitting in it. In any case, this was an incident just waiting to happen.

I try my best to keep my eyes front and forward, which is very, very, *very* hard. To clarify, that refers to me keeping my eyes straight ahead. I twist to open the cubicle door and look left and right to make sure the main toilet is still empty.

'Okay, the coast is clear.'

Still keeping my eyes steadfastly averted to Jackson's forehead, I reach out to him.

'Give me your hands.'

Jackson places his hands in mine – geez, even the man's fingers are firm and strong – and then we engage in a tug of war, with me hauling on one end and Jackson wriggling as much as one can in such a situation. After a few minutes of that heave ho with no success, I decide to try something else.

'I think I need to brace myself to get more leverage to pull you.'

I don't need to say more than that as Jackson readily parts his legs as much as he can so I can brace my foot against the bowl showing between them. As he does this, I can feel a bead of sweat creep down my brow more due to my concentrated efforts to keep my eyes ahead rather than my pulling efforts thus far. Did I say it was very, *very* hard before? Well, I was mistaken. It's that and a few very's more *now*.

Without looking down, I manage to navigate my foot to the vacant space against the bowl but not without my toes first brushing his smooth rock hard thigh. I gulp and blink a few times to get my concentration back to the task at hand.

'Okay, let's try again. On three. One, two, three!'

I brace my foot and pull with all my might with Jackson also trying to push himself in the same direction. Suddenly, he is propelled forward, shooting us both through the open cubicle door, and pinning me against the sink directly in front of it.

'Oomph!' This time that came from me as I stand with my lower back against the sink knowing that what is pressing against my front is not a gun in his pocket.

Jackson quickly lets go of my hands and turns to pull up his trousers. He then turns to give me a hug whilst simultaneously washing his hands in the sink behind me. Hunky *and* hygienic I nod to myself as I reach behind me to do the same thing without turning around. Could this guy be any more amazing? I think I want to have his babies, and Nancy better not object.

'I can't thank you enough, Gina. Dinner is definitely on me now.'

Damn, this man's voice. He should be doing radio commercials. As he looks down on me with those dreamy eyes all I can do is nod like I'm in a trance or something.

'No problem. I think our food should be ready now.'

My legs feel a bit wobbly after my close encounter as I slip back into my shoes. Nevertheless, they get me to the main toilet door without too much of an issue. As we open the door to leave, a man in a baseball cap bumps into me. If seeing me wasn't enough to raise his eyebrows, when he sees Giant Jackson literally casting a shadow over me from behind, he nods his head, gives a smile and pats Jackson on the shoulder as if he is a proud father.

I should rightfully be indignant at that, but all I can think is why couldn't that have been a girl walking through the door to pat *me* on the back. We manage to make it back to our table without further event and sure enough, our meals are ready and waiting on the table. Jackson beckons to the waiter to bring two glasses of wine. I still haven't finished my Virgin Mary but I'm not going to let that get in the way of sharing a glass of wine with this guy. I quickly drain my glass of the remaining contents in time for the approaching waiter to replace my empty glass with the wine filled one. Jackson raises his glass.

'I'd like to make a toast to our shared experience. I've heard relationships based on intense experiences really work.' Jackson holds his glass towards me and I clink mine against it. I don't think it's the right moment to tell him that line from the movie Speed he just quoted was that they never work – especially as I totally want his version to come true.

As I tuck into my chicken wings and Jackson tears into his burger, his deep voice in between mouthfuls is quite hypnotic. I'm not even really hearing what he is saying – just nodding and smiling every now and then in hopefully the right places.

'So what about you?' Jackson asks.

'Erm...sorry, what about me what?'

'Tell me something about you.'

Why would I want to listen to my own voice when I can listen to the voice of this hunk of lusciousness?

'Oh, what you see is what there is.' I smile and then quickly switch the subject back to him. I suddenly feel a bit shivery, like I'm going cold turkey for his voice. 'So, how did you get into Taekwon-do?'

'Well, when I was 12...you know what? You have just seen me with my pants down. Most other women don't get that privilege until at least the third date. I think that qualifies me to miss out some of the normally essential small talk and just cut to the chase.'

Aww man, this does *not* sound like a chase I want to cut to. Why can't he just talk and I just listen? Most men would love that. I take a deep breath and wait. I know what's coming so it might as well be now rather than later.

'I asked you why you were single earlier and I'm still waiting for an answer. I know you must be tired of the question because you no doubt must get asked all the time. I know I do, and my answer is always that fighting is my focus until I meet the right girl. But somehow with you I get the feeling it's more than something like a career. Tell me what you're hiding?' Jackson leans forward and rubs the back of my hand. His smile just makes me forget that I'm supposed to be nervous about revealing this and his deep voice just makes me quiver into submission. How could any woman combat that kind of triple whammy?

'I'm a virgin.' The words just waft dreamily out of my mouth before I even realise it. As soon as the words have left my lips, I seem to snap out of a trance back to reality and freeze in anticipation of his inevitable disbelief. Instead, what I encounter is something that surprises even me.

Twenty Nine

Jackson is just staring at me with an unreadable expression on his face. Then suddenly his eyes well up and a single tear escapes one. I scrape my chair back in shock and then I lean towards him.

'What's wrong? Are you okay?' My concern is evident.

'Are *you*?' And then that's it. The waterworks are in full force as Jackson starts sobbing uncontrollably.

'Uh...oh...stop...er...' I'm in shock. I'm confused. I'm all flustered. I'm everything! I start waving a napkin not knowing if I should dart forward and wipe his eyes before some of his student's parents see him (the ones that he was so concerned about earlier) or wait for him to use his own napkin. He can at least plead that there's something in his eye. It's very possible someone might believe that.

I opt for the one where he sorts out his own tears and slowly draw my chair back in. He reaches for his napkin, dabs at his eyes and muffles his sobs. He then stares at me with those eyes that were once sexy and slitty. They don't seem so appealing now they are red and puffy.

'I'm just so sorry.' Jackson starts sobbing again, biting the napkin.

'Oh please, don't be. It's a sensitive man who can cry in public.' I nod sympathetically. I think this must be a delayed reaction from his toilet saga.

'Not for me, for *you!*' The tears start falling from Jackson's eyes again, 'to have to carry a burden like that? I mean what could possibly have happened for this to happen?' Jackson thumps the table making the unused cutlery jump along with the couple on the next table. The lady gives me a dirty look as if to say how dare you make this lovely specimen of manhood cry. I'm starting to wonder if my secret has maybe triggered some unchartered secret of his – I mean this is extreme in the extreme.

'This is unthinkable. You must feel so...so...I can't even imagine!' Jackson reaches for both my hands, then clambers around the table and envelops me in the biggest of hugs. Which would normally feel *so* good, if it weren't for the added torrential tears drenching the shoulder of my blouse.

'Tell me what I can do?' Jackson clambers back to his side of the table and stares at me earnestly with seriously waterlogged eyes.

I think it's obvious what he could "do" and if this offer had come earlier in the day I would literally have high jumped at the chance. But right now, seeing him bawling and sogging up the place because of what I told him, I'm not so sure. I was SO sure before, but right now I am genuinely spooked by what's going on in front of me.

'I'm fine, Jackson. Really! So don't...erm cry. There, there now. No more tears, okay?' I feel I need to make some sort of physical gesture too, so I reach over and pat him on the shoulder.

'How can you be fine? I mean you are...how old? 34? 35? That is *far* too old to be in a situation like this. How could anyone be okay with that? It's a travesty!' Jackson is sobbing again now, shaking his head and spraying his tears in all directions. Okay, maybe not quite spraying, I know tears don't *actually* spray – but I'm just trying to paint a picture of just how many tears are coming out of this guy right now. I would go so far as to say, the two litres of water he said he drank earlier must be drastically diminished by now. I'd also go so far as to say, I don't think I liked the way he emphasised *far* too old. It's one thing when I say it. He suddenly makes a desperate grab for my arm.

'Have you seen anyone about this? Can I make a donation somewhere to prevent this from happening to other women?'

'You don't need to prevent it from happening. It hasn't happened. That's the whole point.' I give a little laugh trying to make light of the situation but this is clearly the wrong move because that has just set his tears in motion again. This time, Jackson uses his sleeve to wipe his nose – the napkin now being equivalent to a soggy mess. Two women sitting a few tables over have joined the growing list of people staring at us. Sympathetically at him, daggers at me. The whispering has started too and the level of scrutiny being levelled at me from all directions reinforces my guess that I'm the villain in this story.

I'm at a loss of what else I can do or say. There seems to be no end to his tears. I'm convinced that there has to be something else going on with this man.

'Are you sure *you're* okay Jackson? Is there something maybe you want to get off your chest?' And despite it heaving with sobs, what a lovely chest it is. Sigh.

'The only thing I want to talk about is how it's even possible that you have gotten to this stage of your life and never experienced sex.' Jackson says pitifully, the concern in his eyes blurred by as-yet-but-I'm-sure-soon-to-be unshed tears.

I look around hastily. Okay, he really needs to lower his voice. I've not kept this from the whole world for this long for him now to spill it all willy nilly.

'Didn't your parents tell you about the birds and the bees when you were young? Because if they did they would also have told you that birds and bees don't wait this long! I'd say this is tantamount to abuse!' Jackson thumps his fist on the table, making the chicken wing bones jump off my plate. The nearby waiter also jumps out of whatever day dream he was in.

'I think to say abuse is a little strong, don't you?' Okay, he has officially made my list of loopy cray cray, 'come on, does anyone's parents really tell that bird and bee story?' I go for the humour route again, fingers crossed.

'My parents told it to me.' Jackson is straight-faced.

And my attempt to joke my way out of this falls flat again.

'This is just too much for me to deal with right now.' Jackson shakes his head. I'm confused. I thought this was *my* problem to deal with?

'I think we should leave. I need to lie down.' Jackson is still shaking his head spraying me (but not actually *spraying* me) with more tears and pushing back his chair to get up. Geez, who'd have thought this specimen of hunkalishousness would be such a cry baby? Hold on...leave? Did he say leave? Can he not see how many chicken wings are left on my plate to finish? I know I could take them to go but they just don't taste the same reheated. He's right about one thing though. This *is* too much and needs to stop right now and there's only one sure-fire way to make sure that happens immediately.

'Jackson, I'm kidding.'

I don't like to outright lie about my "status" but it just seems the quickest not to mention easiest way to get back to my wings. I never thought I'd have to deny my sexless situation because of a grown man's tears, but then I didn't think I'd be in my mid-thirties and a virgin. Shit happens.

Jackson's tears stop mid-flow and he gives a big sniff and wipes his nose with his sleeve again.

'For real? You're joking? You're not incapacitated in that way?'

I want to indignantly state that I'm not incapacitated at all, least of all by this. But the waterfall of tears that might follow wins the battle.

'Yes. I was just messing with you. You thought I had a secret so I thought I'd give you one.' I wave my hand at him to emphasise this. I can't even smile to add effect. I just feel kind of deflated for some reason. This prime meat steak of a man is not going to be mine. I pick up another chicken wing and start nibbling. It has a somewhat calming effect on me.

Jackson looks at me hard for a minute. One minute stretches into two...I wave my hand in front of his face to see if he is still with me. He blinks a few times, then laughs. I breathe a sigh of relief, that he's all smiles again. But his laughing continues, like *really* continues as in he can't seem to catch his breath.

'Ha, ha ha!' Jackson is rolling back on his chair, holding his stomach as he roars with laughter. I start to laugh a little too, but that soon stops when I see that he can't seem to. He is banging the table, howling with laughter, tears falling from his eyes – again – albeit for a different reason.

'Okay Jackson, it was a little funny I guess. Now moving on...'

But he can't seem to move on. He is holding his ribs and his sexy slitty eyes are beginning to take on a bordering hysterical look. People are starting to stare at us again. The two women sitting a few tables over are part of the staring crew too. This time, I'm getting the sympathetic look and he's getting the crazy guy look. I think to myself, I'm not the villain anymore, yes!

I look back at Jackson, who was going red in the face and is now turning a little blue and can't stop laughing. It is full blown hysterical now and there's only one thing for that.

Thwack! I reach over and give him a hard slap – I've seen it done tons of times in movies and always wondered if it worked. Thankfully, it does and Jackson stops laughing abruptly. I signal to the waiter – who was also staring at Jackson as if he had lost the plot – to bring some water.

'Well, that was a rollercoaster of emotions.' Jackson finally says when he's caught his breath, 'thank you for helping me - again. I suffer from Extreme Emotion disorder.'

You don't say. Bi-polar on steroids or what.

'Shocking news can sometimes bring it on.' Jackson says apologetically, but with that deep voice, even the apology sounds like a love sonnet, 'although I don't know how I could have fallen for that. I should have known such a thing wasn't possible in a million years. That it would have been an anomaly of the first order. That someone like you could never be someone like that...that there was no way...' Jackson continues to inform me of all the reasons as to why someone my age couldn't possibly be a virgin in this day and age while I quietly nibble on the rest of my wings sinking a little more into my seat while I reminisce on how quickly this went from super to super shit. My phone rings and the caller ID shows that it's Cousin Mona.

'Hey Gina, I just wanted to know if I can borrow your car this weekend?'

'Oh my goodness, for real?' I answer with real shock in my voice which is also hopefully showing on my face.

'Erm...yes. It's really not a big deal.' The surprise in Cousin Mona's voice is clear.

'It most certainly is. And I'm coming to get you right now.' I look at Jackson and point to my phone and start to slide my chair back from the table to get up.

'No! I don't need it until the weekend. You don't...'

'Nonsense! I won't hear another word. I'm leaving right now.' I promptly hang up the phone while Cousin Mona is still protesting about something or other. Perfect timing for the perfect excuse to end this not-so-perfect date.

'I'm sorry Jackson. That was my cousin. She needs a ride.' Technically true. I roll my eyes and put up my hand, 'Don't ask. Young people, right?' I shake my phone at him as if that should explain any question he might think to ask.

'Of course! I understand. Thanks again for saving me. Maybe we can do this again without the need for a lavatory rescue next time.' Jackson smiles that tantalising smile again and it very nearly makes me forget that he's the biggest boohoo-er I've ever met. I shake my head back to reality.

'Maybe!' I smile back and turn to go. At that moment a thought crosses my mind. I scoop the last few wings into it a napkin, wrap them up and pop them into my purse, 'waste not want not, my mother always says.' And reheated or not, it would be a sin to waste the last of these wings.

As I head towards the exit, who should be entering the place but Dave. Just my luck. Why couldn't he have seen me a little earlier with that visual perfection of manhood? Then again, he might also have witnessed all the crying and then all the hysterical laughter which I'm sure he would have plenty to say about, all of which I wouldn't want to hear. I raise my eyebrows to him and nod my head in acknowledgement. He gives me a beaming smile I nearly reciprocate. Nearly but not quite. It wouldn't do for me to allow this man to start charming me and then the next thing you know he's buying me underwear from my own shop.

'Don't tell me, another date?' He leans casually against the wall.

'Okay, I won't tell you.' I go through the turning door not sure why that should make me smile to myself. A few seconds later, I want to kick myself as I miss the opening with him watching *again!* Geez, how can getting out of a building be so difficult. Dave raises an eyebrow at me with that same smile as I swing through the door again.

'I meant to do that.' I say haughtily as I swing through the revolving door again making sure that I don't miss the exit second time around. A few steps down the street, I go over the events of the evening in my mind and reach for my phone. Lisa is *so* in for a story telling treat!

***

'Lisa he cried.'

'With laughter?'

'With tears.'

'With tears of laughter?'

'Not at first. At first, with tears of disbelief...?'

'I don't understand.' Lisa sounds baffled.

'He wept.'

'I'm confused.'

'He bawled.'

'Still don't get it.'

'He blubbed. Literally. And *then* he laughed like a maniac.'

'You're saying that hulky, bulky Action Jackson who throws grown men on their arses for a living started crying when you told him you hadn't had sex yet?'

'Yes. And before that, I had to rescue him when he got stuck in the Men's toilet.'

'Okay, hold on a few seconds while I go and get a *whole* bottle of wine.'

Thirty

I've had a bit of a date hiatus for a few days because Lisa is away on some project for work. I really needed the break too, especially after my last date with the crazily handsome, crazily crazy Action Jackson.

I'm actually feeling a bit fed up now too, to be honest. Lisa's plan hasn't quite worked according to plan and it just feels like even though my situation has changed, it's still the same.

I mean, I keep a big secret and that's a problem. I tell people my big secret and it's *still* a problem. An extreme emotion disorder inducing type problem for some. So the bottom line is - I'm no closer to changing my sexual status.

I knew I'd get a shocked reaction from guys when they heard I was green of the sex scene. But what I got was nowhere on my radar of expectation, not even close. I mean outright denial to even consider the possibility that a virgin my age could exist? Buckets of tears followed by frenzied laughter? I mean no one could have prepared for that, not even if they watched a whole series of Don't Tell Me Lies.

Lisa was right about one thing though. It has gotten a little easier to actually say the words 'I'm a virgin'. Flushed cheeks, racing heartbeat, closing eyes in silent prayer that the ground will eat me alive – I've more or less managed to get all that under control. Unfortunately, I've not been as successful when it comes to dealing with the aftermath those three little words conjure up. Sigh. Why doth the course of true virgin-ship never run smoothly?

Okay, enough moping around the house. I think I need to drown my sorrows and what better place than where most of my sorrows have occurred of late. I've grown quite fond of my new local, so need at least one untainted memory of having a drink there. Rymans here I come, for that special cocktail which might as well have been named after me. Literally.

Thirty One

'No date tonight?'

I look around to see Dave hoisting himself up onto the stool next to me.

'Is this your home away from home or something?' I don't mean to sound irritable, but I'm annoyed with life at the moment and he's the only punch bag around.

'Ouch.' Dave jerks his head back as if I smacked him. I immediately feel remorseful.

'Sorry, I guess I'm having a bad day.'

'Why?'

I look at him and he genuinely looks interested.

'You don't want to know why.'

'Yep, I do. Wouldn't have asked if I didn't.'

What I should have said is that I don't want him to know why.

'It's complicated.' I counter.

'Well, I can complete a Rubiks cube and I worked out the storyline of the second Matrix movie first time around. I can do complicated. Complicated is not an issue for me.' Dave gives me a proud look.

'It's stupid.'

'Stupid. Not an issue for me either.' Dave is smiling so easily it makes me smile a little too which in return makes me relax a little.

'If you must know, I've been going on all these dates to overcome a little problem and it doesn't seem to be working out as expected.'

'What's the problem? Maybe I can help.'

If I didn't know that he didn't know, I would be wondering what part of the problem he is offering to help with.

I shake my head and sip my Virgin Mary cocktail, 'I don't think so.'

'Try me.' Dave turns towards me and puts his foot over his knee and swigs some of his beer. I look at him again; this time I *really* look at him. Could I tell him? I mean could his reaction be any weirder than the last guy? Could any body's reaction be weirder than the last guy? Oh, and the guy before that guy.

'Well, it's not a problem in the traditional sense of a problem. It's more something I need to do now which I should have done a long, long, *long* time ago and having to do it now is what's causing the problem.'

'Why should you have done it a long time ago?'

'Because.'

'Because...?'

'Because...it's something that most people would have done a long time ago.' I say most, but I really mean all.

'So you're not most people.'

'But I am!'

'Who says?'

I open my mouth to answer, then stop. That's actually kind of true. Who says I'm most people? And then it dawns on mewho says it.

'Everybody says. Society says.'

'Well, I'm part of everybody. I'm part of society. And I don't say.' He shrugs his shoulders. He's making it sound so simple right now, and it's really not. If it was, I wouldn't be in this situation in the first place.

'You can say that because you don't know what it is. If you did, you'd soon change your mind.'

'So tell me and let's see.' He takes another swig of his beer and just stares at me.

'I can't tell you.'

'Why not?'

'Because you wouldn't understand.'

'How do you know what level of understanding I have? I don't even know until I've heard what it is I'm supposed to understand.' Dave gives me a wicked smile, which on a good day I would probably find charming. Unfortunately, today is not a good day.

'Look, I just can't tell you, okay?'

'If you don't want to tell me that's fine – but don't say you can't – because that's a choice. Just be straight – nothing wrong with being straight.' Dave turns on his stool to face the bar mirror.

'It's not that simple.' I don't know why I'm allowing this man to agitate me. Not everything is as black and white as he might think.

Dave shrugs his shoulders again, 'It's as simple as you want it to be.'

That's it, I've had enough of this exchange, ''I'm a virgin!' I blurt out in a vicious whisper and look around quickly to see if anyone else heard.

I'm expecting Dave to fall off his chair. Or not believe me. Or cry. Or laugh. Instead, all I see is him turn toward me with a raised eyebrow, and even that is only for a few seconds.

'I see. I guess that rather confirms that you're not most people then.' Dave calmly turns back towards the bar mirror with a shrug of his shoulders. He beckons to the bar tender to bring him another beer.

'Did you hear me?'

'Sure I did.'

'I'm a virgin.'

'Yep, that's what I heard.'

'And you really expect me to believe that you don't think that's a rarity at my age?'

'Not at all. I *do* think it's a rarity at your age – what are you? Mid-thirties? In fact, to be honest I think you're the first one I've met – at any age – apart from my niece who is seven' He leans over with an exaggerated whisper from the side of his mouth, 'Remind me to get your autograph later.' He then winks at me before leaning back to his original position, 'but I still haven't changed my mind in thinking that if you didn't want to have sex a long time ago, then you just didn't. End of.'

My jaw is ajar. I look really hard at Dave's profile to see if maybe he's just really good at hiding his true feelings. But other than the raised eyebrow, his demeanour has pretty much remained unchanged.

'You don't think that's an embarrassing thing to admit?'

'You tell me. Are you embarrassed?'

'Yes! Yes, I am!' I have to check myself to lower my voice.

'Why?'

'Why what?'

'Why are you embarrassed?'

'Because...well because I should have done it already!'

'Are we back to that old chestnut again? We've already established that's not necessarily true. I mean hey, it was okay for Jesus's Mum – and she was a Mum. So why are you *really* embarrassed?'

'Because...well because even teenagers who are 14 called Angel know more about having sex than I do! And that can't be right in anybody's world. And to add insult to injury, I sell sexy lingerie that's supposed to encourage more sex. Sex that I, the seller - haven't even tried yet.'

'Firstly, I think any kid called Angel probably has half their future mapped out for them already with a name like that. And personally, I think it would be more embarrassing to be a 14 year old teenager who can recite 20 sexual positions rather than the capital of 20 countries, but that's just me.' Dave whispers out of the side of his mouth again before sipping his beer again.

'There's 20 positions? 20 *different* positions?' I gulp

'You'd need to ask the 14 year old that. I've heard there's a whole lot more but I personally know of – as in use – about nine.

I keep looking ahead so that I don't meet his eyes because I'm not actually sure if he's playing around or not. I sip at my cocktail in disbelief that I've just had a somewhat normal conversation about my lack of sexual experience with a virtual stranger. My very first when you consider the conversations I've had thus far.

I secretly sneak a peek at this guy who is casually sipping a Heineken and nodding his head in time to some cheesy tune that I don't even know (and am quite surprised that he does).

'Well, it was interesting talking to you.'

'Likewise. And if you want to continue this conversation over some food, your assistant has my details so you can pass them on to whoever is arranging your dates for you.'

I open my eyes wide at him, 'What do you...?' I go to deny it then figure what's the point?

'Hey, it really wasn't rocket science. You kind of said as much at the Social Club when you said your peoples wanted you to find a new friend. What else could that really mean? Plus, some of those guys I've seen you with wouldn't have had the balls to ask a girl like you your name never mind out on a date, so I figured they had to have had some help.' Dave takes a sip of my Virgin Mary still sitting on the bar top and screws his face in distaste.

'What do you mean by that? What are you trying to say?' Is he saying I'm unapproachable or something? This concerns me more than him drinking my cocktail.

'Look at you. Look around you.'

I survey the room and notice there are several guys smiling at me. One is licking his lips – ugh – and another one is winking so much anyone would think he's got a nervous twitch. The bar tender gives me a toothy grin – and when I say toothy, I mean I can see fillings and all. A man in the corner is staring at me like he's in a day dream but that gets interrupted by a girl poking him in the forehead. And from the wince he gives and how he's rubbing that head, it must have been the poke of an un-amused girlfriend. I look back at Dave who is still staring ahead into the bar mirror sipping that damned beer. I can't quite think what to say and I don't do speechless very well. And at least he's gone back to drinking his own drink.

'Right...well...'

'Or if you wanted to see me sooner and cut out the middle man, that's okay too. Look, I'll leave it completely up to you – here's my details in case Patsy...I mean your assistant, doesn't have my latest details. I have been known to have rotating phone numbers.' He shrugs his shoulders and slides a drink napkin across the bar at me, leaves a tip for the bar man, winks at me and then he's gone. I shake my head slowly. Did he just ask me on a date but expect me to arrange it? The audacity of the man. However, rather than dwelling on the cheek of this person, I discreetly slip the napkin into my purse. At the same time, I reach for my phone and speed dial Lisa's number.

'Is it that bad already?' Lisa answers straight away, concern in her voice.

'Is what that bad?'

'Your date tonight with Oliver? Don't tell me you forgot! Delilah said she told you it was confirmed. We provisionally arranged this two weeks ago at the meeting for Gregory, your Gran's candidate? I told you to make a note!' Lisa sounds panicky down the phone. I'm not surprised, Delilah will do her nut with both me *and* Lisa if she finds out I stood her friend up. And you really don't want to have to deal with a nutty Delilah if you don't have to.

I can't believe it completely slipped my mind that I'm supposed to be meeting Delilah's candidate tonight. If I don't salvage this she will make it her mission to make my life more hell than she does already.

I look at my watch. I'm already 20 minutes late! Oh no, Oh no, Oh no!

Thirty Two

'No! Of course I didn't forget,' I laugh wildly, 'the date is going swimmingly. In fact, that's what I was ringing to say. See ya!'

I jump off the stool and grab my cocktail but not before the bar tender gives me his number – again. This is the third time he's given it to me, even though two of those times I was meeting somebody. Maybe he has a memory disorder? I take the number – again – smile, and rush to the restaurant area. In my haste, I don't even notice the guy reading the menu next to the men's toilets and head straight into him spilling my drink all over what was seconds earlier, a pristine white shirt.

'Oh my gosh! I am SO sorry!' I make an attempt to wipe the shirt with my bare hands – why? – and proceed to actually make it worse if that's possible.

The guy looks up - at first his expression livid, then when he sees me, it softens almost immediately.

'Oh, don't worry about it. It's fine – look!' The man grabs the glass from me and throws the last few drops in the glass over himself, 'Ta da!' he opens his arms wide like a magician.

'This old shirt needed a splash of colour in it anyway. Feel free to spill your drink over me anytime. In fact, here's my number. Maybe you can spill it over me at dinner?' He winks at me and then holding the wet shirt as far away from his body as he can, he goes into the men's toilet.

I know he said the shirt needed a bit of colour but I don't think that was quite the truth. I push his number into my bag and make a mental note to call – to offer to replace the shirt (because it will never be that pristine white again) not spill another cocktail over it - then resume my rushing to the restaurant area.

I still can't believe I forgot a date that Delilah arranged of all people. That should have been super glued in my memory. One thing I do know -she'll make sure I never forget this if she ever finds out because I'll never hear the end of it! I reach the food area and am straining my neck to catch a glimpse of this guy and my phone rings. I answer it without looking at the caller display.

'Hello?'

'Really? You are standing up *my* candidate? Do you know how much persuading it took to get a guy who has only ever really wanted to date me for years, to consider going on a date with a stand-in?'

Did she really call me a stand-in? For her?

'This is my reputation on...'

'Delilah. Calm down. I am simply running a little late. I will be with Herb...'

'It's Oliver!'

'Oliver! Oliver. I will be with him in like 30 seconds, okay?'

'See that you are. You are the consolation I have offered to Oliver after five years of having to deal with losing me to Paul. Let's not forget I'm also giving you much needed help finding someone willing to settle for you. The least you can do is turn up in a reasonable time and with better hair than you had when I last saw you.'

'Excuse me, but...Hello?' She hung up! She's insulted my hair and just hung up without even giving me a chance to defend Justin's debut into hairdressing. So what if one side is longer than the other? It's not like it will stay that way for ever, tch.

I get to the restaurant area and there are four guys wearing carnations. Damn, we need to go with Chrysanthemums as the new identifier. Who knew carnations was the go to flower for recognising dates? Two of the carnation guys are waiting tables so unlikely they'd get set up on dates in the middle of a work shift. One of the other two is wearing a sateen suit with a gold sheen to it, jet black spiky hair and two very crooked front teeth. Delilah would never admit in a million years that a guy who wears a suit like that is besotted with her so that definitely rules him out. That leaves the fidgety guy perching against the edge of the table over there with the very straight nose. In the thirty seconds I've deduced that he must be Delilah's candidate, he has used hand sanitizer three times. I walk over and offer my hand to shake.

'Oliver? I'm Gina. Sorry I'm late.'

He looks me up and down for a few seconds, then gives me the world's briefest handshake before crossing his hands behind his back. I think that's meant to be his discreet way of non-discreetly sanitizing his hands for a fourth time.

'Shall we sit?' I say. He nods and produces a wet wipe from nowhere like a magician and wipes off the seat.

'So Gina, Delilah said you were having problems finding someone to go out with you and that she thought we might hit it off.' Oliver crosses one leg over the other, then brushes off a spec of something he notices on his shoe.

'Really? She said that?' Does that woman never miss an opportunity to mee-ow?

'She did. And looking at you, I do find that a tad surprising.' Oliver tilts his arrow straight nose at me.

'That's because that's not exactly correct, but hey, shall we order drinks?' I hand him a menu which he takes from me and goes over with another wet wipe.

'Hmm...I *already* ordered an ice tea. I'm detoxing.' Oliver emphasises the "already" to not so subtly remind me that I am late. Like I needed it. I just smile and let the comment drift into the atmosphere. The waiter is soon back with Oliver's ice tea and another Virgin Mary that I funnily enough hadn't actually ordered yet, but welcome with open arms.

'I do suspect that Delilah has used tonight as a reason to contact me again. She took it quite hard when I broke up with her five years ago.'

I splutter my drink at the sound of this, 'Sorry? *You* finished with Delilah?'

'Yes. I was going abroad to finish my studies in America – I'm an actor you know - and a long distance relationship would have been too distracting.' Oliver dramatically sips his ice tea – imagine what *that* looks like if you can.

'I see.' It's so hard to hide the smile inside me right now. I'm gonna load this ammunition into my memory and shoot that cow in the face with it the very next time she is insulting to me. I can't wait for her to tell me my arse is too big again. Just can't wait! Oliver links his fingers as they rest on the table and just stares at me. The intensity of it is starting to make me feel a little uncomfortable.

'Is something wrong? You're staring. Like *really* staring.'

'Sorry!' Oliver laughs for the first time tonight, 'It's just that you are nothing like Delilah described you.'

A normal response would be to ask how she described me – but it's Delilah, so it wouldn't be brain strain to guess.

'I find it hard to believe that you are not already with someone, Gina.' He shakes his head in disbelief and sips his ice tea. Not so long ago, I would have greeted that statement with apprehension. But I think I'm in a place right now – especially after speaking so easily to Dave – where I can execute Lisa's plan without too much discomfort.

'It's because I'm a virgin.' I say calmly. I mean he can be shocked or not believe me, right? I think I'm prepared for that now. I know Dave's reaction was neither of those and that he is the exception, but I'm worldly enough now to deal with the rule.

Oliver is doing that staring thing again, but this time even more intensely, if that's possible. Then he slowly reaches over and pokes me as if to see I'm real, before quickly pulling back his hand.

'Ouch!' I rub where he's poked and then glare at him.

Suddenly he looks horrified and actually gives a sound resembling a scream as he scrapes his chair back to move away from the table holding a pristinely starched hanky to his mouth.

'What? Where?' Startled by his reaction, I put my hands up in a defensive Kung Fu stance that I saw on last week's episode of Nikita and look around to my left and right to see what he's so aghast about.

'You! That's what. What do you mean you're a...you're a...*virgin?*' He closes his eyes and swallows hard to force the last word through his lips, placing his open hand against his chest.

'Is it contagious? Oliver harshly whispers at me.

'Huh? Is what contagious?'

I am – in a word – confused.

'You haven't done "it". That's what you said, right?' Oliver takes out his hand sanitiser and sprays it on his hands and then sprays some at me!

'Hey, what are you doing?' I wave away the spray of liquid, 'what are you implying?' It's hard to hide the incredulity from my voice.

'It must be medical right? I mean you own a sexy underwear shop.' He nods to himself like that explains everything. He comes closer again, 'Is it like Chlamydia? Or something more exotic?' he whispers harshly.

'What? No! It's not! I don't have an STD! How can I have a sexually transmitted disease if I've never had sex?' I only just manage to not end that sentence in 'Duh!'

'Oh...that's right...silly me!' Oliver looks relieved, and then he seems to have another thought, and puts his hanky to his mouth again with a questioning look.

'But you're 35 aren't you? No one gets to 35 and hasn't had sex by choice. It's just not the done thing...unless it's not a regular one... is that it?'

'Is that ...what?' Might have known Delilah would try to foist one of her crazies onto me.

'You know...'

'Err...no, I don't.'

'Is your vejayjay not normal?'

'My vejay*what*?' Is he asking...what I *think* he's asking?

'You know...has it been touched by the freak fairy?' Oliver points down to my private parts. I don't think I could have gotten redder if I was sunburnt. Oliver is pacing up and down the length of the table. He then takes out an asthma inhaler and starts pumping into his mouth.

'Were you part of an experiment? To see how long someone can stay "that" way?' Oliver is standing a good few feet apart and holding out his hand like he is trying to ward me off! He then looks thoughtful, 'that might not be a bad idea for a script. I should call my agent...'

'Of course I'm not an experiment!' For goodness sakes!' I am too annoyed to even be shocked.

Abruptly, Oliver points his finger at me accusing-ly.

'Why are you walking around like this,' he waves his finger at my nether region, 'is it okay? You should be quarantined or something! Can you imagine if I caught what you've got and regressed two decades to be like you are now? I couldn't do love scenes with my leading ladies – as talented an actor as I am, I couldn't fake my way through,' he points to my nether regions again, 'that.'

I don't think his leading ladies would mind as much as he thinks – I mean, he's no Action Jack-son, not by a long way. Oliver is now crossing both his hands against his chest. He couldn't look more horrified if he tried. He suddenly throws his hands high in the air.

'I simply can't afford to get what you've got. Just being in this very vicinity could ruin my career. You know what? I don't think I should be around you. That,' he points to my vejayjay for a third time, 'might be able to jump cross species.'

Oliver edges through the gap behind my chair and the table behind me, careful not to touch me. So now I'm either a diseased alien or diseased ani-mal – I don't know which one is worse. Actually, if

I add his acting into the mix, *that* would definitely win.

'I can't believe Delilah would expose me to something like this. She knows I'm filming next week in Dubai.' He mumbles under his breath but I can still hear him clearly through the tissue covering his mouth, even from three tables away. He puts the back of his hand against his forehead, sighs to the sky, then like the Flash, he's gone.

I am stunned. What happened just now? It doesn't even get time to sink in properly when my phone is ringing again. I absently reach for it. It's Delilah.

'Delilah, who on earth…'

'What did you DO?!!' I have to hold the phone away from my ear before her screeching tone does my eardrum some serious damage.

'Excuse me? What did…*I* do?'

It's not me she should be asking that question to!

'Or what did you say then?'

Her accusing tone just makes me respond in the same way.

'Excuse me? What did *I* say?'

This time I add a little more emphasis.

'Oliver just called me on the phone, practically hysterical saying how could I put him at risk like that and he thought we were friends. I went to a lot of trouble – a *lot* – to help you find someone and you ruin it. You probably deliberately sabotaged the date so don't think I won't report this to Lisa so that you can pay your forfeit...'

'What? What forfeit?'

I've never heard of any forfeit?

'You'll find out soon enough, I'll make sure of that!'

The dialling tone in my ear tells me she has hung up. Has the world gone mad? I take a few minutes to let this all sink in. I then go to dial Lisa's number and she must have read my mind because my phone is ringing again and it's her.'

'Lisa, you really need to get a better vetting process in for these dates.'

'Geez, what happened? I've just had Delilah on the phone bending my ear!'

'I don't know what happened! I followed the plan, told him what I was and his reaction was not one we rehearsed.'

'What do you mean?'

'He poked me like I was from outer space then acted like I had the plague or something!'

'Are you serious?' The shock in Lisa's voice vibrates down the phone.

'Like a heart attack.'

'Gina, I am so sorry that you had to go through that. Are you okay?' Lisa's voice switches to concerned.

'I didn't have time to not be okay – it was over before it could even register.' I think about what I've just said. And I really am okay. Still no embarrassment or cringeworthy-ness. If anything, I feel like I want to headbutt somebody – Oliver – for associating someone delaying having sex with being at deaths door. I guess that pre-chat with Dave freed my mind even more than I thought.

'Just wait - I will personally give Delilah and her loopy candidate a chunky piece of my mind. It will not be pretty. And to think she had the cheek to demand you pay your forfeit when *her* guy was at fault.' Lisa tuts down the phone

'Actually, what is this forfeit? This is the first I've heard of a forfeit? I didn't agree to any...'

'Hey. Consider your forfeit forfeited, okay? I've got you. See you later hun!'

'Wait...Lisa...' But she's gone – conveniently, I'm sure. Anyhow, a forfeit is the least important thing on my mind right now – something else is suddenly more pressing.

Thirty Three

Oliver was the last straw. In an instant, I have decided that I am not executing Lisa's plan with any more of these Head cases, nor dealing with any more of their extreme responses to my little tale. If I didn't think I was normal before, I sure do now. These dates I've been on have brought it home to me that I'm definitely not the abnormal one.

I dig into my bag and take out the napkin with Dave's number on it. I stare at the swirly written digits and start tapping the numbers out on the phone. I don't press dial though. Instead, I clear the screen. I stare at the napkin for a bit longer and then do the same thing again – tap the numbers out then clear the screen. This happens a few more times before I shove both the phone and the napkin into my bag, down the rest of my Virgin Mary in one, and leave the table.

As I hit the streets, I'm having a conversation with myself in my head. One side is saying you could just talk to him about your situation knowing he's not going to burst into tears or think that Nancy has been touched by the freak fairy. The other side is saying he buys underwear for different women every week. Apart from being a really good customer, do you really want to share your innermost thoughts with someone like that?

A thought hits me – what's important here is that I get over this hurdle. I'm a 35-year-old virgin who really needs to get her bread buttered if she wants to move on in her relationship life. Nothing else really matters right now. I stop dead in my tracks, causing a woman to bump straight into me, dislodging her spectacles. After profusely apologising, I pull out my phone and the napkin. This time I tap out the numbers, tap dial and don't hang up until I hear 'Hello?'

Thirty Four

It's a week after my last diabolical date and I still haven't told Lisa that I arranged my own meeting with a guy tonight. It was really last minute and I know it will probably mess up the dating time table she has for me. I couldn't bear for her to have to redraw all those columns of information – especially as she pressed so hard on her ruler last time that she snapped it.

I've already had a female version – Lisa's – on how to get my apple cored. I think I just need a male point of view now as to how I can get to that next stage so to speak. No more testing-the-water dates with loopy cray cray people. Now I've considered the possibility of a normal sexual life that I don't have to keep secret, I just need to do 'it' already.

I reach what I now regard as my local and push round the revolving door of Rymans. I look over to the bar area and Dave is already there, perched on his regular seat. He waves to get my attention. He then points to the carnation on his shirt and opens his arms. I cannot help but laugh.

I walk over to the bar and slip onto the stool next to him. The barman straight away brings me a Virgin Mary cocktail and places it in front of me with his customary wink and yet another piece of paper with his number under the glass stem.

'I took the liberty' Dave says and clinks the glass with his bottle of beer.

'So I see.' I take a sip of my drink and discreetly crumple the bar tenders number. I started to feel a little nervous as I was approaching the bar, but now I've seen him, my nerves are gone.

'You know this isn't a real date, right?' I confirm to Dave.

'Well, I'd at least like to think of it as a semi date. I've bought you a drink and I'm wearing a carnation so I've fulfilled enough pre-requisites for that, I think.' He cocks his head to the side and I laugh again.

'Okay, a semi-date.' I smile my agreement.

'So, what's on your mind?' Dave takes a swig of his beer.

'Well, further to our last conversation about my...situation. I told a guy and his reaction was extreme to say the least. Not one I've encountered before.'

'He's an idiot.'

'I haven't even told you how he reacted yet.'

'It doesn't matter. He's still an idiot.'

'But...'

'Idiot.'

'I suppose he...'

'Idiot.'

'Well, it is...'

'Id-i-ot. Full stop.'

I am exasperated now, 'So what does that mean for me? I need to move forward, and it's difficult enough without having to deal with...idiots.' I slump down in the stool. I have to blink back tears of frustration.

'Okay, let's start at the beginning. What's really going on with you about being a virgin?'

'Well for starters, it's embarrassing.' I don't even need to think about that answer.

'Were you embarrassed when you told me?'

'Well...no, not really. Felt like we were talking about the weather. Almost.'

'Were you embarrassed when you told the idiot?'

'Then, I was more shocked. I mean, he acted like I was an alien!'

'Are you an alien?'

I punch him on the arm, 'Of course, I'm not.'

'What about when you told Lisa? Were you embarassed then?'

'I was more concerned that she hadn't broken her neck! When I told her I think she fell off her bed in shock!' I shake my head at the memory of hearing Lisa's phone hit the ground...and then her after.

'Well, that sounds like if there is something stronger than the embarrassment at play, then that replaces the embarrassment. I think you just need a distraction at the moment of truth.'

I think for a minute, 'A distraction?'

'Yeah, I think so. Talking about something totally unrelated. Watching a thriller. Even a change of scenery, might help shift your focus from the actual embarrassment of it all.'

I just stare at Dave and he stares back and shrugs his shoulders. I stare in front of me, deep in thought. Could it really be something as simple as a change of scenery to get over this thing?

Geez, I feel like I'm in a session with a shrink. Now I see why they charge so much money.

'And then it's obvious how to deal with that.'

It is? Dave sounds like he has the answer to this whole thing. But in my mind, there's no way he can arrive at a solution so simply. I've been dealing with this for years – there's been nothing simple about it.

'And what way is that, then?

'You need to be in the right setting.'

Huh? 'Care to elaborate?'

'Well, if you are in the right setting then you'll feel comfortable or relaxed or excited or whatever but embarrassment won't be your focus. One thing will lead to another, you'll start having fun and before you know it, it'll probably be over. That happens with a lot of guys – I'm not one of them I might add.' Dave gives a cheeky smile. I roll my eyes at him, but give a little smile too. Could it really be that simple?

'Sooo...what do you think would be the right setting?'

'It's not what I think, it's what you think. It would be wherever feels right for you.'

Hmm…I guess I'll need to give that some more thought as it's not something I've ever considered before.

'Hey, is eating allowed on a semi-date? Because I am starving.' Dave starts to waver on his seat as if he is going to faint with hunger.

'I guess there are no hard and fast rules on a semi-date, so why not? I'll meet you in the restaurant area, just got to pop to the loo.'

Dave jumps off the stool to go bag us a table. On my way to the loo, I text Lisa:

```
Me: Forgot to tell you - on a
semi-date
```

```
Lisa: Oh! Not sure what that
is, but I'll put it on your
schedule. I want full details
when it's over! xx
```

I smile at the message and push the door into the toilet. I instantly recognise the two girls at the sink as the two I spoke to before when I gave advice that I couldn't swallow myself when it related to me.

'Hey!' Both girls say to me with big smiles. Candy, I note is in another interestingly short dress/top.

'Hello, how's it going girls?'

'Good! Oh, remember that guy we were talking about last time? I told him I needed to wait and he was okay with it! I could hardly believe it, you were right!' Tina – in an equally short dress/top grabs me in a big hug.

'I think i'm ready to do it now! But I don't know where my first time should be?'

Candy pipes up, 'I said it should be somewhere exciting, like in a helicopter!'

'And I think it should be somewhere grand like in a castle.What do you think?' Both girls are staring at me as if the next words I utter will be made of gold. And suddenly it becomes clear to me.

'It should be somewhere you feel comfortable or relaxed or excited. Your setting should be wherever feels right for you.'

'Ooh, you're so right.' Both girls say together and leave the toilets in a big discussion about where the best place would be.

I'm sure Lisa will have plenty to say on that – not that I'm saying she's done it in a million places or anything – but I haven't even done it in one, so

I don't have a clue what might be a good place for your first time.

As I top up my lipstick, I still can't believe that I'm going to have a conversation about where to "puncture my tyre". And with a man who buys underwear for different women on a regular basis of all people – who'd have thought? A customer and a confidante!

In any case, if this means Nancy won't shut up shop anytime anyone comes a knocking then it's worth a try. And if not for Nancy, then for me and the chance of a proper date with someone that hasn't been picked by the 3Fs.

But baby steps for tonight as there is hope on the horizon that I'm gonna one day get onion pickled! Maybe I'll choose chicken for my meal tonight too, as this is one time I don't think I'll need the chewy beef!

THE END ...of *this* part ;-)

Gina's Back!

Now that Gina has let her secret out of the bag, it's
time to put it to bed – literally!
But is 'bed' the best place...?
Wouldn't a beach be more romantic?
Or maybe the kitchen table for spontaneity?
There's only one way for her to find out!

And only one way for YOU to find out too!

And that's in:

The Perfect Place

(The BIG Secret – Part 2!)

Available Now!